Caterpillars Can't Swim

CATERPILLARS CAN'T SWIM

LIANE SHAW

Second Story Press

Library and Archives Canada Cataloguing in Publication

Shaw, Liane, 1959-, author
Caterpillars can't swim / by Liane Shaw.

Issued in print and electronic formats.
ISBN 978-1-77260-053-7 (softcover).—
ISBN 978-1-77260-054-4 (EPUB)

I. Title.

PS8637.H3838C38 2017   jC813'.6   C2017-902845-6

C2017-902846-4

First published in the USA in 2018

Edited by Kathryn White and Kathryn Cole
Design by Melissa Kaita
Cover © iStock.com

Printed and bound in Canada

*Second Story Press gratefully acknowledges the support of the
Ontario Arts Council and the Canada Council for the Arts for our
publishing program. We acknowledge the financial support of the
Government of Canada through the Canada Book Fund.*

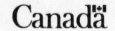

Published by
SECOND STORY PRESS
20 Maud Street, Suite 401
Toronto, ON M5V 2M5
www.secondstorypress.ca

For Jamie

You left us long before we were ready to say good-bye.

Now all we can do for you is dream.

"NO ONE CARES IF IT'S
A BOY OR A GIRL.

IT'S JUST A CATERPILLAR
THAT CHANGED INTO A
BUTTERFLY.

AND IT'S OKAY AND
RIGHT AND NORMAL."

ONE

"Go!"

Steve's voice shoots straight into my back, pushing me off the starter block and into the water. Arms, head, and body stab the surface in perfect alignment, slipping in silently like a knife into a jar of the disgustingly oily natural peanut butter my mother always buys, even though we like the unnatural kind better. Legs follow the crowd, slapping the water like they're pissed off at it and making a splash that I know drives Steve crazy every time he sees me do it. I don't care about him though. All I care about is the water holding on to me so that I can push myself to the limit. It's cool against my face, and I can feel my swim grin starting. Steve always tells me that the grin makes it seem like I'm not taking things seriously enough and that I should try to look more like the other guys on the team. Since most of them have their faces all scrunched up like they're trying to take a painful shit in the deep end, I'm sticking with my own expression.

Besides, I am serious.

I *seriously* love being in the water. All of my parts decide to cooperate once I start to swim, and I basically forget about the whole world. All I can feel is my body moving fast and furious like an underwater street racer…arms slicing, thighs pumping, and lungs holding in air until I feel like I'm going to explode and go flying right into the other end of the pool.

I can't hear anything but the blast beat rhythm of my own heart pounding. I know that Steve is up there somewhere, yelling his face off, telling me that Peter is coming up on my ass, or that my left arm isn't moving the way it should be. When I finish my laps and he tells me I wasn't listening for the millionth time, I'll just blame my earplugs like I always do, and he won't believe me but he won't bug me about it either.

Steve treats me like everyone else when I'm in the water, but the minute I'm on dry land, he usually has a lot more trouble bitching me out than the other swimmers.

Most of the time it bugs me when I'm treated differently from everyone else, but sometimes it's an advantage.

Avoiding Steve's locker-room lectures is definitely one of those times.

"Peter, what the hell was that turn? You took twice as long as everyone else coming out!"

"Miguel, you need to get off the block faster and cleaner. Understand?"

"Cody, your strokes weakened halfway down the first lap. You're supposed to pick up speed, not lose it!"

Steve stomps up and down between the benches like some kind of frustrated drill sergeant from one of those stupid army movies my dad likes to watch, stopping at each guy's locker and yelling in his face while he's trying to dry off and get dressed.

Steve takes being a swim coach very seriously. He doesn't ever grin.

I'm already dried off and mostly dressed by the time he finishes making everyone else feel like yesterday's garbage. By the time I'm back in my chair, Steve has usually headed back into his office. Sometimes he nods at me when he walks by.

Most of the time he just walks by.

I can't prove it, but I think my chair makes him nervous. When I'm in the water, he can forget that I come to school in a handicapped bus and spend my days wheeling around the hallways trying not to run over anyone's toes.

Handicapped bus. As if it somehow isn't as big and strong as all the able-bodied buses.

Our school's about a hundred years old and not designed for human bodies, let alone wheelchairs. The halls are so narrow that the principal actually painted a white line down the middle so that everyone will stay in their own lane at class-change time. I don't fit inside the white line so some of my teachers give me a head start at the end of class so that I can wheel down the hall by myself.

Because being alone is always *so* much fun.

We live in a very small town, and I'm the only person in

my school who lives in a wheelchair. They actually had to build a ramp for me when I started there so that I could get in the front door. I have to use the staff bathroom because the cubicles in the kids' ones are too small for my chair. When I started at the school, I was told they'd be renovating as quickly as possible so that I could be part of the social experience of pissing with the other kids. That was three years ago. Pretty sure I'll be graduated before they do anything.

I don't think it's affected my social skills in any significant way, and I'm used to it by now, although Cody likes to helpfully remind me on a regular basis that I'm sitting in the same place that probably just held the bare ass of someone who can give us a detention. I try not to think about it.

When I was really young, I don't think I realized that I was different from anyone else. I was a little baby and people carried me around the same way they did with all the other little babies, so I fit in just fine. Then when I was a bigger baby, I started to crawl. My thighs and knees worked pretty well, so it didn't really bother me that my calves and feet didn't seem to have any strength in them and liked to twist around at strange angles without my permission.

When I was around two, I figured out a way to walk fairly upright. I just stood on my knees and ignored the bottom half of my legs. I could move around everywhere I wanted to go. I was fast, too, and pretty cute. My mother has the proof in about fifteen videos she has saved on her computer that she likes to embarrass me with on a regular basis.

It wasn't until my baby brother arrived on the scene that I

started to figure out that something wasn't quite right. It's not as if I'd never seen another kid or anything. My parents took me to parks and stores and all the other normal places that people go. I guess I just never really paid attention to what other kids were doing. Maybe I thought that kids in my house walked on their knees and everyone else used their feet. I don't know.

But when Ricky was born, it all changed. Not right away, but it didn't take very long. By the time he was around a year old, Ricky could walk straight up on his feet and legs. He was taller than me on my knees by the time he was eighteen months. Faster too.

My parents and doctors had tried to get me up on my feet, but no matter how much physio I got, I never could catch my balance when I was on my own. My lower legs would twist over each other and trip me up. The bigger the rest of my body got, the less helpful my skinny little calves were in getting me moving. I could move a little if I was wearing special braces and holding on to a walker, but I had to concentrate so hard on getting my lower legs to cooperate with the rest of me that I kept forgetting to hold on. Then I would fall over like a tree that just met up with a chain saw.

My parents finally took pity on me when I was at home and got me some kneepads and just let me do my thing most of the time.

I got my first wheelchair when I was almost five.

My parents tried to tell me how lucky I was to have my very own chair with wheels—how special it was to be the only kid in my class with my own vehicle.

I don't remember if I believed them or not. I'm not sure if I cared. The chair was comfortable enough, and after some practice I could move pretty fast.

My mom started me in aquatic therapy around the same time that we got my chair, and I fell in love with the water instantly.

Gravity was no longer my enemy, and I could move around like anyone else. Even though my kicking was literally spastic when I first tried to get my thighs to bring my calves and feet along for the ride, I gradually figured out my own system. I could feel myself getting stronger every time I dropped into the pool.

At first I only swam when we went to the city, where I had my therapy sessions in the big pool at the Children's Hospital Rehab Center. But as I got older and better at it, my parents decided to try me in regular swim lessons at the community pool in our town. The teachers were pretty nervous around me at first. I'm fairly certain I was the first kid in a wheelchair they'd ever actually come in contact with. They seemed pretty uncomfortable with the sight of my chair at the side of the pool and even more freaked out when I pushed myself out of it and onto the edge.

I still remember one of them kind of shrieking a little the first time he saw me roll into the water. It was pretty funny. I also remember laughing as I surfaced and then waving at the guy before I took off swimming to the far end of the pool.

Maybe that's where my swim grin came from.

TWO

We practice for swim team before school three times a week. That means getting up at five o'clock and literally dragging myself out of bed, and then not so literally dragging my mother out of her bed so she can drive me to the pool. My dad gets to snore through the whole thing because he commutes to work so he has to be rested enough to drive. Mom is the principal at the local elementary school. Apparently you don't need to be rested to supervise a couple of hundred kids.

On the days in between, I still wake up at five o'clock no matter how hard I try to persuade my mind and body to stay sleeping. Most days I can't make myself go back to sleep so I just lie in bed imagining graphic novel plots. I know obsessing on graphic novels makes me some kind of teenage-nerd stereotype, but I can't help it. I think the stories are cool and the drawings are art in its purest form.

My best friend, Cody, is an even bigger nerd than I am and even has an action-figure collection, which he keeps a secret from pretty much everyone but me because, well, basically they're little plastic dolls that he's afraid to play with in case he breaks one. That might seem cool when TV characters do it, but it's not something you want to share with too many people in the real world—if you want to keep your face intact. At least, not in *our* real world.

On days like today, when I wake up at five o'clock and can't think up any interesting story lines and I don't want to do anything else like worry about my next math test, I get out of bed and head down to the water. Our town might be small and seriously boring most of the time, but it *is* actually really nice to look at. Tourists come here from the surrounding cities all the time, just to look at the old buildings and to sit by the river.

There's an old wooden bridge that crosses part of the river not far from our house. It's barely wide enough for my chair to cross when it's empty, and most of the time it's full of bikes and people. But this early in the morning even the joggers are still in bed, so I like to head down there and just sit on the bridge and look at the water. I sit up and reach over to turn on my light. I transfer myself into my chair and wheel into the bathroom that my dad renovated so that everything is easy to reach and there's lots of room to transfer from my chair to the toilet or shower. I take a quick shower and then get dressed, shoving my legs into their braces before putting on my shoes. Even though I can't really walk on them, my legs still sit better if they're held in place by plastic and Velcro. I have to rub my feet to relax them enough so that they stop fighting me and let me fold them into the bottom part of the braces. I stick my shoes on over top. I know that shoes seem kind of stupid for someone who doesn't walk, but it's surprising how many things bump into me or drop on me during an average day.

I head for the front door, easing it open so that I don't wake anyone as I wheel out onto the front porch. I reach back and close the door as quietly as I can. It's already warm outside, which means the day is going to be brutal at school. The only places in the school with air-conditioning are the library and the main office. Apparently books and administrators need to stay cool while the rest of us just get to sweat and stink up the place until it smells like the barn at Cody's farm.

The bridge is only a three-minute coast down the street from our place. It's shaped like an arch, with railings that were painted red once upon a time but are now peeling like my back after a bad sunburn. For most of the ride over, there's a railing helpfully positioned exactly in front of my face so that I can barely see the water. But there's spot about three-quarters of the way over where a piece has broken so that the wood hangs crookedly toward the bridge floor, giving me a "window" down to the surface. Since I can't get my chair down to the actual shoreline, this is where I sit and just stare at the water.

I usually sit for about a half hour, or until I hear someone panting their way across the bridge, trying to get in some early morning jogging. As soon as that starts, I'm gone.

It's beautiful here.

I wouldn't say that out loud when Cody is around because

he would say I sound like a girl or gay or something. Cody is a nice guy and a good friend most of the time, but he's like a lot of the guys I know around here—pretty much homophobic, relatively racist, and always saying things about girls that he thinks are funny but would make my mother royally pissed off. Your basic small-town triple threat.

Not that I'm saying *everyone* here is like that. They aren't. It's just that it seems like this town is frozen in time and a lot of the attitudes around here are stuck in the ice. My mother says she spends a lot of her time at school working on thawing out the attitudes of the kids so that someday things will be different.

I don't think it's working yet.

I spent a lot of time with city kids at the rehab center growing up and quite a few of them seem to have different ideas about people than the kids here do. My mother says that it has something to do with the fact that cities are a lot more diverse than most small towns, and that it's easier to learn to accept people you perceive as different if you actually see them in person and find out that they're not so different from you after all.

I don't know if she's right or not. One thing I'm pretty sure of is that everywhere you go, you can find some racist, homophobic, misogynistic jerks who like to stare at people in wheelchairs like we've got a contagious disease.

Anyway, it *is* beautiful here. The river stretches right across the town, kind of winding its way off into the distance, disappearing into the trees that line up on either side like leafy green gargoyles standing at attention.

I like gargoyles. I have a novel plot in my head that features a couple of them who sit on top of our school during the day and then come to life at night so they can defend the rights of students who get picked on by assholes.

The shoreline has been left alone, so it's completely natural with tall grass that almost looks like a wheat field and millions of wildflowers that look like something out of a painting. There are all kinds of birds flying around the trees, and the ducks and geese float proudly on the water, as if they own the place.

I wish *I* owned the place. I'd force everyone else off the bridge and just keep it for myself. I'd ask my dad to help me build a ramp so that I could get down to the water and maybe figure out a way to get in there and swim without chlorine.

I check my watch. Fifteen minutes gone. I'll stay another ten then head back. I actually do have a math test today so I probably should take a few minutes to do something useful like study for it. Not that it will help much because I seriously suck at math. Mostly because I hate it. I'd rather be reading or swimming or pretty much anything other than trying to figure out why I should care what *x squared* plus *y squared* equals.

I really should go back now. Mom will have a fit if I fail another test. She has some idea that math is important to my future. I don't see how algebra is going to help me. The only thing I'd ever be using math for is keeping track of my swim times, and I can already count and tell time.

I reach over to release the brakes on my wheels so that I can force myself to go home, when a movement catches my eyes. Someone is down by the water. I can't really see who it is, but it looks like a girl dancing around in the flowers.

That's something I've never seen here before.

She's twirling around like some kind of ballet dancer putting on a show, throwing her hands up in the air and kicking her feet up after each twirl. She's wearing a bright yellow skirt thing that floats up every time she moves in a circle. I think she's singing but I'm not totally sure.

I watch for a while. The wind catches the skirt and swirls it up higher, which makes it interesting for a couple of seconds until I realize that she's wearing jeans underneath it. Nothing to see there.

I shake my head a little, wondering who she is and why she's dancing around like a crazy person at five-thirty in the morning. Of course, she likely thinks she's alone, so I probably should stop sitting here like a stalker and give her some privacy. I reach down and unlock my wheels, then move forward to the end of the bridge so I can turn around and head back over to my house. I glance toward the flowers but I can't see her anymore. I sit for a second wondering about her before heading over the bridge again.

When I get back to the hole in the railing, I take one last look at the water before heading home. And that's when I see her again.

In the water.

THREE

She's in the river, water up to her chest. I can see the skirt floating around her, making a strange swirl of color just below the surface. Why is she trying to swim with so many clothes on?

What the hell is she doing?

"Hey!" I try shouting to get her attention, but she just keeps moving forward. She's almost directly under me now and the water is up to her chin. In a second she'll be in over her head. I know the water is pretty deep right there because lots of kids like to jump off the bridge in the summer to cool off and I've never heard of anyone cracking their head open in that particular spot.

"Hey!" I reapply my brakes so I don't roll back. I'm leaning forward, trying to see her better. She doesn't look up at me when I shout.

13

"Hey! What are you doing?" I'm screaming at her, straining to see what she's trying to do.

Suddenly I can't see her at all.

Has she gone under?

She must have.

I wait a second, expecting to see her surface and start swimming. I can see movement under the water. At least I think I can. People naturally start to swim when they get into deep water. It's a survival thing. She should be surfacing any second.

I watch and wait.

She isn't coming up.

Why isn't she coming up?

I watch for a few more seconds. I think I can still see movement, but her head doesn't break the surface. This is crazy. No one stays under that long on purpose.

What am I supposed to do?

"Help! Someone help!" I scream it at no one, fear clawing at my throat as I start sliding out of my chair. I get down onto the ground and push up onto my knees, moving forward into the space made by the broken railing. I get to the edge and brace myself as if Steve is standing beside me yelling that it's time to swim and telling me to stop being such a wuss.

But it looks really far down. I think I can see where she is, but I can't tell if she's still moving or not.

I don't know what I'm looking at.

I have to do something!

"Help!" I scream it again, so loudly that I'm pretty sure my throat has started to bleed, and I push off, smashing my way toward the water. All four limbs immediately fly completely out of control as I try to use my thighs to pull my lower legs up into some kind of safe position.

God, I hope I don't land on her!

I smash into the water, and it punches back at me, filling my mouth as I go down. I fight my way back to the surface and spit it out so I can fill my lungs with air. I take a deep breath and dive down, swimming around in circles, hoping I'm somewhere close to where she went under. I can't see anything. I don't have my goggles and even if I did, the river is a lot murkier than the nice chlorinated pool that I wish I was in right now.

I can feel the panic bubbles filling me up like some kind of rapidly decompressing scuba diver. My thighs are kicking, but it's hard because I have my braces and shoes on and they're weighing me down.

I can't think about that. Can't think about going down. Concentrate on staying up. Floating. I'm in the water. I love the water. It's my friend. It keeps me up and lets me move. It won't hurt me.

I'm on the swim team. We won the county championship last year. Steve would tell me to stop whining and swim.

I would tell Steve to shut up.

I really want to whine because I'm scared shitless. How long has she been under? One minute? Three? How long have I been under?

I grab at anything that comes into my line of pseudo-sight, but it's mostly seaweed. I keep grabbing and grabbing until suddenly I feel a handful of what seems to be fabric. Praying it's her skirt, I pull on it, hoping that I'm dragging myself toward the rest of her. My lungs feel like they're on fire, and I want to breathe so badly that I have a sudden urge to just open my mouth and let the nice cool water put out the flames.

I fight the urge away as I finally I brush up against her and manage to grab her arm. I twist my body and get one of my arms around her in the recovery position and start to pull her along as I head for the surface. We're not very far down, and I quickly break both our heads out of the water and suck in as much air as I can. I look to see if she's doing the same thing, but she just lies back on the surface, still and quiet, which probably means she's not breathing at all, but I don't really know for sure. I've only ever done lifesaving in training sessions in the pool with someone who's pretending to be drowning and is usually laughing the whole time while Steve yells at us. I don't know what someone looks like when their breath has really gone away.

I swim for the shore, putting everything I have into it. I have to move my legs as fast as I can so that I don't sink us both, and my thighs hurt like hell. My muscles are screaming at me to stop moving while my mind tells them to shut up and just keep going. It feels like it's taking forever, but I don't really have any idea how much time has passed.

I get to the edge of the river and pull myself out of the water, digging my fingers into the ground, trying to get turned around onto my knees so that I can move. I drag her up onto the ground beside me. She's not moving at all. She's definitely not breathing, and I don't know when she stopped or if I can get her started again.

I have to do CPR but I'm shaking, and I'm not sure if I remember how to do it. I start compressions but I'm trembling so much I don't know if I'm putting enough pressure or too much or if I'm even on the right part of her body. This is totally different from pretending with Cody while he makes puking noises every time I lean over him.

Compress.

Check.

Definitely no breath. When did she stop breathing? How long before it's too long?

Breathe for her. Am I supposed to do that? I can't remember!

Scream!

"Help. Someone help!"

What's the order? How many compressions am I supposed to do? I really can't remember anything!

"Help me. Please!" Maybe if I'm polite someone will come running.

I keep going and going. I don't know if I'm doing it right. I don't know if she's been out of air for too long. I don't know anything. It all just goes on and on until I'm starting to feel like I'm running out of air too, and we're both going to end up lying in the grass, passed out or worse.

And then suddenly, unbelievably, she coughs, just like in the movies. Just a little at first, but then she starts making choking noises as she struggles to sit up.

"Are you okay?" I ask, which is unbelievably stupid because she obviously isn't.

She opens her eyes and looks at me for just a second, and then they close again. I start another dose of panic until I realize that the cough seems to have jump-started her breathing enough that she's still going.

Okay. Good. She's breathing. Now what?

We're still here alone. No one heard me.

I'm going to have to get myself back up onto the bridge and find my cell phone so I can call 9-1-1. I look up at my chair. It's a long way from here. I don't know if it's safe to leave her long enough to go and get it. What if she stops breathing again? Can that happen? Can she stop again once she's started? What's safer? Waiting or going?

I scan the bridge as best I can from down here. I can't see anyone. I don't know what time it is. It could be an hour before someone decides to start their morning run.

I can't just sit here. I have to get up to my phone.

I check one more time to make sure her breathing is steady enough that it feels safe to leave.

That's when I realize that I recognize her.

Except that she's not a *her*.

She's a *him*.

FOUR

Shit!

I was freaking out so completely that I didn't even notice the chest I was pushing on belongs to a guy.

Jack…Paterson, or Petersen. Something with a P. Doesn't really matter.

Not just a guy, but someone I know. He's actually in the same grade as I am, but we don't share any classes this year. He was in my math class in grade nine though, and I think we were in the same grade six class and either grade seven or eight, too, but I'm not sure which. We're not friends or anything, but I know him to say hi or whatever. I think we were in the same science group for a project once. Maybe not. I don't know!

I stare at him for a few moments, catching my breath and steeling myself to figure out how to get back up onto the bridge.

What the hell is Jack doing here? Why does he look like this?

He still has on the long yellow skirt that's now all wet and muddy. He's also wearing jeans and running shoes. Running *shoe* I should say, because one has disappeared. His foot looks sort of small and sad lying there without its shoe.

A sad foot. Stupid. My brain must be soggy.

He's wearing a jean jacket over a T-shirt. His shirt is moving up and down so I know he's breathing, but he still isn't conscious.

I have to get up onto the bridge to grab my phone. I push onto my knees again and take a deep breath, looking up at my chair. It's been a long time since I've "kneed" it that far, and I'm a lot heavier than I was back then. It's going to hurt. A lot. I wish I still had those kneepads. The ground is bumpy and so steep, it looks like a ninety-degree angle to me. Geometry… my mom would be so proud.

I start to move away from Jack and then stop, looking at him again. I don't know for sure what he was trying to do wandering around in the river at sunrise, but it's obviously nothing great. I don't know why he's wearing a skirt either. Obviously I know that there are guys in the world who like to wear what most people figure are girl clothes…but not around here. Guys in our town have a pretty strict dress code.

As in no guy would ever be caught dead in a dress.

Shit! That was a stupid thing to say, even to myself. My brain needs to shut itself up.

I reach down and pull the skirt off of him, rolling it down from the elastic waist and tugging it off from under his feet. I wrap it up into a tight, soggy ball and shove it under my arm.

I don't know why.

I start moving through the tall grass, which keeps scratching my face and going up my nose, making me sneeze. The hill feels as steep as it looks and is full of rocks that bite me with every movement forward. My knees start to hurt almost instantly, but I do my best to ignore it, channeling tough Steve to get myself up to my chair.

"Hey! Are you all right?" The voice comes at me from above, and I look up, eyes watering and snot dripping down my chin. Jack is lying behind me, wet and still.

A woman dressed in full jogger's uniform is standing beside my wheelchair on the bridge, looking down at me. She's obviously not the most observant person in the world but still someone who likely has a cell phone and can call for help.

"No! Call 9-1-1!" I scream it, my voice shooting out at her like a stray bullet, sounding totally panicked, which doesn't make sense because I should be relieved now that someone is here. I roll off my knees and sit for a second. Now that help is coming, I probably should head back down to where Jack is, just in case he stops breathing again. Although I'm not sure if I have enough air left to do anything to help him if he does.

Up on the bridge, I can see the jogger on her cell phone. She'll be jogging down here in a second.

I take the soggy mess out from under my arm and shove it under a bush, pushing it back out of sight. I have a feeling that Jack isn't going to feel like explaining the skirt once he wakes up.

Although I don't really know him so I could be wrong. But if I am, then this is the right direction to be wrong in, I think.

I don't know!

My mind is definitely waterlogged. I can't get my thoughts straight. I just need to get moving and try to stop thinking.

"Oh my god, are you all right? Is that your chair? Can I help you? I called the police. Someone will be here any second!" Her feet and voice both come crashing at me through the grass. She's beside me before I make it back to Jack.

"I'm fine. You need to check him!" I wheeze it at her because I'm trying to move fast on my now bloody knees.

"What happened to him?" She shouts at me as she runs by.

"He fell in the water. I don't think he can swim. I did CPR." I do my best to shout back. She says something that I can't hear and kneels down beside Jack, laying her hand on his chest.

He fell in the water? Where did that come from?

"He's breathing!" This time I hear her, the words acting like brakes as I just stop and fall over on the grass. Once I'm stopped I notice that I hurt. My knees hurt. My chest hurts. My head hurts.

Steve would tell me to toughen up. I would tell him to shove it.

Well, not really. But I'd want to.

My mom will be up by now and wondering where I am. She knows I go out for a spin sometimes in the morning, but she doesn't know I come here. She'll be worrying soon. I should have kept moving uphill to my phone.

"Can I do anything for you?" The jogger is standing beside me. She glances back up at my chair and then stares at my legs for a few seconds until she notices me watching her do it.

I can hear sirens coming down Main Street. We don't hear a lot of sirens here. Everyone will be wondering what's going on. It will be the most exciting thing that's happened around here in weeks. *Yay.*

"I need to call my parents." I push myself back up to a sitting position so that I won't seem so pathetic. I wipe my hand across my face and look down at my knuckles, which are now totally covered in my own grossness. I was going to ask to borrow her phone, but she might not be too happy to share at the moment. Maybe she didn't notice.

"Oh, right. Of course. What's the number? Here, I'll dial it for you."

She obviously noticed. I give her my house phone number as I try to wipe my hands off on my wet pants without making the mess worse. "Don't worry about that. It's fine," she says, smiling as she takes pity on me and hands over the phone.

My mom answers on the first ring. I try to explain the basics to her while the sirens fill in the background at an ear-piercing level that makes it almost impossible to either speak or hear. The sound finally dies down as the cars stop at the bottom of the bridge. I hear the slamming of car doors and then several cops come running down the hill. I have to tell my mother that I need to get off the phone so I can talk to the police.

I'm pretty sure the next feet I hear running over the bridge will be hers.

The next few minutes are filled with more noise and confusion. The paramedics arrive about two seconds after the cops and head down to Jack. They stop by me first but I wave them on. I watch them checking his vitals and loading him onto the stretcher. He still isn't conscious, which is weird. In the movies, once they cough, it's all sunshine and happy thoughts and leaping to their feet, cured and ready to fly.

"That's your chair?" I look up, shielding my eyes from the sun, which has decided to join the party. Good. Maybe it will dry me off a little and I won't look so pathetic when my parents show up. I squint up at a policewoman standing there sweating in full uniform.

"Yes."

"Okay. I'll get the paramedics to send another team to help you back up into it."

"I don't need paramedics. My parents will be here soon." I just get the words out of my mouth when I hear my mother yelling from the bridge.

"Ryan! What happened to you? Are you all right! Jason! He's down here. Hurry. I think he's hurt!"

My parents both come running down the hill so fast that they're stumbling by the time they get to me. My dad is still in his pajamas, and my mother is wearing sweat pants and a wrinkled sweater that she must have grabbed out of her laundry basket. Her face is as wet and snotty as mine. Mom's always been a crier.

She crash-lands beside me and grabs me in a giant hug.

"Lynne, let go of him. We need to check that he's not hurt

before you smother him." Dad's voice comes into the craziness, calm and controlled like it always is. Nothing much freaks my father out.

Mom immediately lets go of me and sits back. "Are you hurt?" she asks.

Yes! Everything on me hurts.

"No. Not really. Just my knees are sore and my shoulder from hitting the water the wrong way," I answer in my manliest voice. My dad likes me to be cool like him. Which I am… out loud, anyway.

My mother takes a Kleenex out of her pocket and starts cleaning my face. So much for manly.

"Let's just get him back up to his chair. I think he needs a hot shower more than a Kleenex," my father says quietly.

"I'll get an officer to help you," my mother says, looking up at the steep hill. My dad can transfer me easily at home. I can put some weight on my legs if he's holding on to me. But carrying me up a hill is a whole new deal.

"I don't need any help. I'm fine!" Dad practically shouts it at her as he gently eases me up and into his arms. My dad is not a yeller, especially not at my mother.

I'm turning seventeen this year. I'm soaking wet and wearing my braces. I'm pretty tall although most people don't know that. I am not exactly a lightweight.

Dad carries me up the hill, holding me close like I'm four years old again. A cop comes over to help, but Dad manages to wave him away, stomping through the grass, puffing and panting like our dog when he sits too close to the firebox. I'm afraid Dad's going to pass out, but I'm even more afraid to tell him to stop. He has a strange look on his face that I think is saying *shut up and let me do this*.

It also could be saying *my kid is an idiot*, but I can't be sure. Either way, he seems pissed, and I don't know whether it's directed at me or not.

He gets me back to my chair and stands for a second, hugging me so tightly that I feel like I might literally stop breathing.

As he finally places me gently into my chair and steps back to catch his breath, I realize that no one has actually asked me for any details about what happened yet.

I guess the fun is just beginning.

FIVE

So maybe *fun* isn't exactly the right word for it.

I thought everything hurt when I was sitting beside the river. I was wrong. That was just the preview of the actual pain that I was going to feel after my shower. By the time I manage to get in and out of my bathroom, my shoulder is threatening to detach itself from my body, and my knees are so raw I'm sure I can see my kneecaps through what's left of my skin.

My father comes into my room and after one look at me sitting there all bloody and bruised decides that a shower was just the beginning of what I need. He loads me into the car, along with Mom, and we all head to the hospital to make sure the paramedics didn't miss anything.

The doctor checks me over and says my knees were just scraped up badly, but there isn't any actual damage to the ligaments or anything else I might need. He isn't one of my regular doctors and he kind of looks at me strangely when he says it, as if he's wondering why a kid in a chair would be worried about his legs anyway.

Then again, I could be projecting a little because every tiny piece of me has started to hurt and I'm feeling supremely sorry for myself.

"The shoulder is a different matter. There is some tearing of the ligament that will need some decent healing time. We'll have to immobilize it for a while to make sure that the healing happens."

"Immobilize it? For how long?" I have to struggle to control my volume.

"A few weeks, give or take. We'll have to check it regularly and figure it out as we go. You were lucky. It could have been worse. I'll send the resident over to bandage up that arm." He smiles and wanders out into the hall.

"That's not too bad," my mother says, sniffling a little. I hope she doesn't start crying again. She cried when we got home. She cried when she saw my bruises. She cried when we came to the hospital. She must be getting dried out by now.

Not too bad? This is bullshit! I can't do anything without my shoulder. I need it to move my chair. I need it to swim! What am I supposed to do?

My mother is smiling at me hopefully. My father is staring at me, eyebrows scrunched together, looking as if he's waiting for me to say something.

I keep my mouth shut. I'm too tired to come up with a happy lie. Mom will just get more upset if she knows I'm pissed, and I can't handle any more tears. My dad looks relieved at my silence and his face smooths out. I don't think he likes crying any more than I do. He gives me a tiny smile and shakes his head a little.

The resident comes in to bandage me up. My arm is pressed against my chest in a tight sling. I can't even move my own chair now. I'm definitely immobilized.

At least I'll have to stay home from school until my shoulder heals. After all, my mother always tells me to look for the bright side in every situation.

"We'll have to look into renting an electric chair so you can stay mobile at school." My father wipes out the bright side with a big black cloud of Dad logic. Great plan. Electric chairs are likely even bigger than my manual one. I can take up the whole hall instead of only three-quarters of it.

"Do you think they'd tell us how the other boy is doing?" my mother asks as we head for the exit.

"I'm not sure, but we could try asking about him," Dad answers, looking at me with his eyebrows raised, making it a question. I'm surprised for a second but then quickly nod. I've been so busy feeling sorry for myself for the past couple of hours that I more or less forgot about Jack. Well, actually just more. I haven't thought about him at all. That's amazingly awesome of me.

"Excuse me, Mr. and Mrs. Malloy? I'm Officer Peabody. I was wondering if we could speak with Ryan before you leave… assuming he's up to it?"

The police officer interrupts my dad's walk over to the

reception desk. I think it's the same woman who talked to me at the river, but I can't be sure. Everything is starting to blur together in my memory, and the details are disappearing into a pile of mush.

"I suppose so. Ryan?" My father raises his eyebrows at me again. I never really noticed how expressive his face is before. He can really make those eyebrows talk.

I really don't want to talk to the police right now with any part of my face. I think I should talk to Jack first, even though he probably doesn't want to talk to me.

I have a bad feeling in my gut that I know what Jack was trying to do, but I don't want to be the one to talk about it to the cops.

"I actually wanted to see Jack while we're here. I'm feeling pretty tired, though, so I'm not sure how much I can handle right now." I give the cop my best pathetic poor-little-kid-in-a-wheelchair face as I put a bit of a hitch in my voice. I'm pretty good at making people feel sorry for me when I don't want to do something.

The cop looks all sympathetic and nods. My father closes his eyes and shakes his head. The pathetic, kid-in-a-chair routine does *not* work on family.

"I can understand that. Perhaps I could come by the house later this afternoon, once you've had a chance to rest. You deserve it. You're quite the hero. You saved that boy's life. You'd better be prepared for some media attention."

"Thanks, Officer. We're pretty proud of him." My mother smiles and extends her hand. They shake, both looking at me as if I just discovered the cure for the next pandemic that would've wiped out humankind.

Hero? Me? I hadn't thought about that part of it. Maybe I should write a graphic novel about myself.

"I've already been in with Jack. He's awake but not ready to talk to anyone…at least not to me. He might be more interested in talking to a friend. I'll see if I can arrange it." Officer Peabody heads over toward the reception desk without waiting to see if anyone thinks that's a super wonderful idea.

Awesome.

I really handled that well. I figured the cop would just go away and then we'd find out that Jack isn't up to visitors and we could go home. Now I got myself stuck inside of my own lie. Even though I know I should talk to him, I don't actually *want* to talk to Jack right now any more than I want to talk to the cops. I'd rather wait until I'm feeling less like screaming every time I move. Well, to be honest, I'd rather wait forever but I don't think that's an option.

This is not going to be pretty. If anyone thinks he's going to shout "My hero!" when I walk into his room, they're probably going to be surprised. He's more likely to tell me to go to hell.

I don't even know him. I'm the last person on earth he's going to want to talk to. He wasn't there at five in the morning because he wanted witnesses.

"All right. I spoke with the nurse and she said it should be fine for you to go in with him for a few minutes. Your parents can wait in the cafeteria. I'll bring you back down to them when you're done."

Oh good, Officer Peabody is on the case.

"If he's too tired I can just do it another time," I say, trying to make the words sound sympathetic instead of like a lame excuse to delay the inevitable.

"No, I think it would be good for both of you. But we have to go right now before he falls asleep again." She doesn't wait for me to answer, but just grabs my chair and starts wheeling me toward the elevators. She's not a very patient person.

I hate being pushed in my chair. I like to be in control of my own movement. I'm not a fan of electric chairs but it'll be better than this.

We ride the elevator up to the fifth floor, staring at ourselves in the mirrors that are plastered across the walls. Why would anyone think that people in a hospital want to stare at themselves? You're either sick or visiting someone who's sick. Not exactly a good hair day either way.

My hair isn't looking so great. I forgot to brush it after my shower and it's sticking out all over my head like some kind of orange-flavored porcupine. Most people call me a redhead but that's just a polite way of saying my hair is bright orange. After all, I'm not different enough rolling around in a town full of bipeds. I have to look like a moving traffic cone, too.

I want to smooth my hair down, but I don't want Officer Peabody to notice me doing it. I don't want her to begin a conversation and try to find a clever way to start questioning me. I don't have any answers ready yet.

I decide to ignore my hair and close my eyes. That should stop any conversation attempts. I don't open them until the elevator stops. The doors open and I get pushed out into the hallway. I feel like I'm being forced to go somewhere against my will, even though I'm the brilliant guy who said I wanted to do this in the first place.

I don't want to see Jack. I don't know what to say to him. The guy's obviously pretty messed up. What am I supposed to do? Do I let on that I saw the skirt and that I took it and hid it under a bush, even though I had no idea whether or not he would have wanted me to do that?

Or do I just keep my mouth shut and let him think…I don't know…that it fell off in the water or whatever happens to skirts when you wear them in the river?

I don't want to talk to him, but I don't want to talk to the cops either. I know they want to understand what happened, but I feel like this is Jack's private business. After all, he wasn't hurting anyone.

Anyone *else.*

This all sucks. I should have stayed home this morning and studied for my math test.

SIX

"Here we are. I'll take you in and be just outside."

Officer Peabody doesn't bother to wait for an answer and just whips me into the room and parks me beside Jack's bed. I think she needs to cut down on her caffeine intake.

Jack is lying all tucked up under the sheets, his face so pale that he seems to be blending into the fabric. He's awake, eyes open, just staring up at the ceiling. He doesn't seem to notice that I'm here. I look around the room a bit and that's when I realize there's a woman sitting in a chair over by the window. Her eyes are closed and she has a book open on her lap. I assume she's Jack's mother. She doesn't seem to have noticed I'm here either.

I sit silently for a minute, wondering again what I'm doing here. Jack isn't moving. Maybe he's sleeping with his eyes open, which is creepy on all kinds of levels.

Am I supposed to just start talking and wake both of them up? What do I say? *I caught your show earlier?* Probably wouldn't be a good start. Something simple like *How are you?* I think I know the answer to that one.

"Oh, I didn't notice you come in. You're Ryan!" The woman at the window jumps up, knocking her book onto the floor. She comes over to the bed and looks down at me. Her eyes are full of tears. Another crier. I wish Mom was here. She could handle this better than I can. Kindred spirits, or whatever.

"Yes. Hi." It feels like I should be talking in more than single syllables, but I can't get my mouth and brain working together. Jack still doesn't move at the sound of our voices.

"I don't even know what to say to you! How do I thank you?" The tears are streaming down her face now, and she looks like she wants to hug me but can't figure out how to do it.

"You don't have to thank me. I just did what anyone would." I should have stuck to single syllables. Now I sound like I'm on some crappy TV show.

"Of course I have to thank you! The police say you saved him. He's never been a strong swimmer. I can't imagine what he was doing so close to the water. The police said you told them he fell. I don't know how that could happen." Her eyes turn it into a question.

Jack's head turns a little on his pillow. I glance at him. Now he's staring at me instead of the ceiling. His eyes are so dark that his pupils seem to have blended into the iris. He's staring without blinking, and I have to look away before I get sucked in to one of the black holes.

His mother's eyes are also dark brown, with lots of red in there too. She's obviously been crying a lot. I wonder how much she knows.

"I don't know either," I tell her. "It all happened so fast. I just saw him in the water and my swim training kicked in." I sort of answer her question, still sounding like a badly written character on some dramatic movie of the week.

"Well, you're my hero. Jack's too," she says, looking over at him. I glance as well. He's still staring at me. I don't think those eyes are saying *hero*.

"Anyway, I'm going to go and get something to drink. I'll let you boys talk. You can buzz the nursing station if you need anything." She leaves the room before I can answer. I guess everyone's in a hurry today.

The room is silent. I hope that Jack decides to go back to memorizing the ceiling instead of trying to psych me out with his eyes. I glance back in his direction. Shit. He's still staring. Doesn't this guy ever blink?

"Why?"

The word is quiet, just above a whisper, and I almost miss it.

"What?"

"Why?" He says it a bit louder this time. I don't know what he's asking me. Does he want to know why I saved him?

"It looked like you were drowning. I couldn't just sit and watch."

"No. Why did you say I *fell?*" I barely remember saying it.

"I…just…didn't know what to say. I guess. I wasn't sure

what really happened." That's almost true. One second he was there and the next he was under water.

"You saw me?" He looks back up to the ceiling. I know what he's asking this time.

"Yeah."

"Did anyone else see?" His voice is trembling a bit. It makes my throat hurt.

"No. Just me. I took your…um…stuff off and hid it."

"Why?"

Again with the *why*.

"I don't know. I thought you might not want anyone to see it or something. Just a guess." I shrug my shoulders, which makes one of them move and the other one scream in pain. I bite my lip so I don't join in.

"Okay."

I don't know if he's telling me that what I did was okay or if he's just ending the conversation. I can't think of anything else to say so I just sit there. He obviously can't think of anything either because he just lies there. After a few moments of nothing, Jack closes his eyes. I figure that's my cue to leave so I reach for the buzzer to request my escape. His hand whips out and grabs my wrist, making me jump.

"What will you tell the cops?" He's staring at me intently, holding my wrist with really strong fingers. This guy is seriously creeping me out.

"I don't know. I guess it depends on what they ask me."

"I don't want anyone to know. Not yet, anyway. Just keep saying I fell off the bridge. An accident. Whatever. Just for now. Please?" His eyes start to fill up just like his mother's did. I nod my head quickly. I can't handle any more full on crying today.

"Yeah. It's cool. I'll just say I saw you in the water. That's mostly true." Leaving pieces of the truth out isn't exactly the same as lying, is it?

He closes his eyes for a second and nods, taking a deep breath in and blowing it back out like he's practicing how to breathe. He's still holding my wrist in a vise-grip and I try to gently pull back. His eyes fly open and he looks at me, tightening his fingers even more. This kid is stronger than he looks, and it's starting to hurt.

"Do you think caterpillars can swim?" he asks in a serious voice that makes it seem like the most important question in the world.

"What?" What the hell is he talking about? Caterpillars? Who gives a shit about caterpillars a few hours after almost drowning?

I think it's time for me to go. I really need to press that buzzer thing, but now both my hands are immobilized.

"Never mind." He whispers it as he shakes his head slightly and gives my wrist back to me. His eyes close again, and he turns away. One tear breaks loose and rolls down his cheek.

My throat is really starting to ache. I hope I'm not getting sick on top of everything else.

I quickly press the call button, hoping that Officer Peabody doesn't waste too much time taking me back to my parents. At least I turned my lie around and can tell her the truth if she asks again. I'm definitely too tired to handle any of her questions. I just want to go home and sleep.

By the time we do get home, there are all kinds of messages on our answering machine from people wanting to talk to the new town hero, telling me how wonderful I am, and thanking me for saving Jack's life. My cell phone is full of texts from kids at school, and Cody sent a message telling me to check out his Facebook post about me because he thinks it's going to go viral. As if.

Everyone's saying how amazing it was that I was at the right place at the right time.

I'm pretty sure Jack would disagree. I'm pretty sure he thinks that I was in the wrong place at the wrong time and that I should have stayed in bed this morning so he could do what he really wanted to do without anyone there to stop him.

I don't want to think about it. I just want to go back to bed and start the day over again so I can pretend none of this ever happened.

SEVEN

Officer Peabody must have caught a case actually involving a real crime or something because she ended up leaving me alone for a while. I had hoped that the whole world would also leave me alone so that I could hide in my room for another week instead of going back to school, but my parents had a different idea.

"I was thinking that Cody could help you out until we get the other chair. You've been home a whole week, and it would be good for you to get back to school," my mother says, as she walks into my room without knocking, an annoying habit she's redeveloped since I did my swan dive off the bridge. I had her trained to stop doing that years ago, and now I'm going to have to start over again.

"Cody? You want to have Cody push me around school all day? Seriously? You have met him, right?" I'm staring at my mother as if she just grew wings and a stone tail.

Wings. A pair of those would be pretty useful right now.

"Of course I have. He's your best friend. And I know he's a little…energetic, but he means well, and he'd be happy to help you, I'm sure."

"Energetic? Try completely hyperactive. The only time Cody can channel it is in the water. The rest of the time, the guy is literally bouncing off the walls. He'll be bouncing *me* off the walls if I let him push me around school."

When I was a little boy, my mother used to read me Winnie the Pooh books. My favorite character was Tigger, and I loved it when my mother sang the bouncy song to me. Cody is a complete Tigger doppelgänger. Maybe that's why I liked him in the first place.

"I think you're exaggerating, Ryan," Mom says, shaking her head.

"You can think whatever you want. Last week, he slid down the railing on the main staircase and almost landed on Mr. St. Clair." Mr. St. Clair is our VP. He's a real tough guy and doesn't take crap from anyone. He wasn't too impressed when Cody came flying at him feet first. Cody is still in detention every day. He might be in detention until we graduate.

"Ouch!" Mom scrunches up her face and starts to laugh. "I don't imagine Philippe was too happy with that. I used to teach with him about a hundred years ago. He's never had much of a sense of humor." She wipes her eyes a little and shakes her head.

"Sense of humor? No. I don't think I've ever even seen him smile. Anyway, Cody is not an option. Maybe I'll just stay home for a few more days." I try a sweet smile and puppy dog eyes.

"You look like you're going to throw up or something equally gross." Ricky walks into the room and throws himself down on my bed.

"I think he was trying to look persuasive," Mom tells him, ruffling his hair and grinning at us both. "It didn't work. Ryan, you need to go to school. We'll figure something out. Maybe Ricky…"

"No!" We both shout it at the same time. Ricky is two grades behind me, and we do our best to ignore each other at school. Having him push me around would be almost worse than Cody. My mother holds both hands up, pushing the word back at us.

"Okay, okay. I get the point! I'll talk to Dad and see if he can put some pressure on the rental place for the other chair." Mom leaves the room. Ricky looks at me for a second.

"You want something?" I ask.

"No, not really. Everyone's talking about you at school."

"I know. All the hero crap. Cody's been keeping me posted."

"Yeah. Everyone thinks it's so amazing that a guy in a wheelchair could save someone. Kind of stupid."

"What do you mean?"

"I mean, it's stupid to be so amazed that someone on the swim team could save someone by *swimming*." He rolls off the bed and stands over me. "I don't think you're all that amazing."

"Good to know, you little shit." I smile pleasantly. He grins.

"Anyway, now that you're a hero, maybe you can get a girl to like you."

I grab the closest thing I can find and throw it at his head. Unfortunately, the closest thing I find is a paperback novel, so it doesn't really make much of an impact. Ricky laughs at me as he ducks.

"Good thing you didn't try out for baseball. You seriously suck!" He runs out of my room, ducking again as I try to up the ante with my math textbook. I miss him again. He's right. I do seriously suck at pretty much every sport but swimming.

And now I can't swim until this stupid shoulder heals. If it doesn't do it fast enough, I'll be out for the whole term.

This situation sucks on every possible level.

Except the level where Jack didn't drown.

Ryan the hero.

I don't even know for sure that I saved him. I don't know that he wouldn't have figured out a way to swim if I'd just left him. Maybe jumping in there like some X-Man wannabe actually made things worse and I almost drowned him before I had to save him.

I haven't talked to him since that first day in the hospital. There are all kinds of rumors floating around about him, which is one of the reasons I'm not really excited about going back to school right away. I don't want to answer any questions. I figure if I wait a while to go back, the wondering might die down a bit and I won't have to talk about Jack.

I'm also hoping that the cops will lose interest or forget about talking to me so I don't have to talk about Jack to them either.

I wonder how much they suspect. I don't think anyone

really believes that he just randomly fell off the bridge into the water. It would be pretty hard to do by accident unless you were standing on the other side of the railing, on the very edge, and leaning forward without holding on.

Pretty much you'd have to jump on purpose to get from the bridge into the water.

So even if I say what Jack asked me to, I doubt anyone is really going to believe me.

Cody told me that everyone at school thinks Jack tried to *off* himself. Cody's words, not mine. He said that people think Jack was depressed or in trouble or on drugs or abused or whatever other possibilities they figured out from watching too many cop shows on TV.

My guess is that no one has the slightest idea what happened or why.

Except Jack.

I have the *slightest* idea but I'm not telling anyone. It's none of my business. It's Jack's business.

That's what I keep telling myself. But it feels like it's a little bit of my business too. I'm the one who pulled him out. I'm the one who hid his stuff.

His *secret*.

How he is going to go back to school? His life is obviously already a screwed up mess. How the hell is he going to walk into the rumor festival and keep his shit together?

Jack Pedersen. I keep trying to pull some thoughts about him out of my brain but I don't know who his friends are or if he does any sports at school. I can sort of see him sitting in math class, a couple of rows over from where my chair and I park at the side of the classroom. I'm trying to remember if I ever saw him talking to anyone or laughing or anything that would make him into a real person inside my head.

Mostly all I see is his black eyes trying to pull me into some kind of endless pit of nothingness.

That's a good line. I'm going to use that one when I start writing my novel. Maybe that's what I should do instead of going back to school. I'll write a famous novel that will make me so much money that I can quit school and just write and swim for the rest of my life.

Once my shoulder gets better. Can't type much any more than I can swim with only one arm. My whole life feels like it's immobilized by this stupid sling, plastering my arm to my chest.

I wonder if that's what Jack feels like. Immobilized. Stuck at home trying to persuade everyone that he didn't try to do what everyone thinks he did.

Hiding under the bushes along with his skirt.

Shit.

"Mom!" I yell. I hear footsteps move quickly down the hall.

"Are you all right?" She runs back into the room, looking worried.

"Yeah, sorry. I didn't mean to yell so loud. I just wanted to get your attention and…" I stop talking at the sound of the bell ringing in my face. My mother has this antique school bell that she keeps on her desk. She brought it home so that I could call her without shouting while I'm waiting to get mobile again. I keep forgetting about it. Mostly because I think it's stupid.

"Right. The bell. I'll try to remember. Anyway, I was wondering about something."

"Sure. What is it?"

"I was thinking that maybe I should go and see Jack. He doesn't live far from here. I just thought I could…check on him, I guess."

"I think that's a terrific idea," she says enthusiastically. I can't tell if she's faking it or is actually as excited as she sounds. I think she has some weird idea that Jack and I are friends.

"Okay. Good." Or not.

"I'll just give Mrs. Pedersen a call and make sure she's all right with us coming over. I wrote her number down somewhere. I think it's in my purse."

Us. Of course. My mommy has to take me over to Jack's because I can't get there myself. Like some baby being pushed in his stroller.

Shit. I hate this. I'm starting to like the whole electric chair idea more and more. Hope it gets here soon even if it means I have to go back to school.

Mom calls Jack's place and reports back that "they" are thrilled with the idea of my visiting my best friend, Jack. Pretty sure that "they" doesn't include Jack.

The house is only a ten-minute walk from our place, which is a good thing because my mother seems to feel the need to perform a running monologue about everything she sees along the way. I guess she's trying to keep me entertained the way she used to when I was a baby and she really was pushing me in a stroller. Fun.

"Here we are," Mom says redundantly as we get to Jack's front door. She rings the bell, and after a few seconds, Jack's mother answers.

She looks so tired. Her eyes seem smaller than before, as if they're disappearing into her face.

"It's nice to see you again, Ryan."

"Hi, Mrs. Pedersen," I say quickly when my mom gently pokes me in the back.

"Hello. I'm Lynne Malloy." Mom shakes hands with Jack's mom, pumping her arm up and down so hard that I'm afraid she's going to break something.

"It's Alison. Come in, please." Jack's mom steps aside as Mom pulls me backwards into the house, over the small doorstep. She plasters a giant smile on her face, which makes her look a bit like a gargoyle grinning before a feast. Mrs. Pedersen looks at both of us with sad eyes, her mouth moving slightly as if it's too tired to remember how to smile.

I try to imagine how my mom would react if I had been the one being rescued instead of doing the rescuing. She's upset enough that I ended up in the water as it is. I actually can't imagine how she'd be acting if she thought I'd been trying to do something to hurt myself on purpose. She hasn't said anything at all about Jack and how he got into the water. She hasn't asked me one question about it. I don't know if she's giving me space or if she doesn't want to think about the answer.

"Jack's room is just down the hall." Mrs. Pedersen starts

walking, and my mother pushes me along behind. We stop at the second door on the left and everyone looks inside the room.

"Thank you for bringing Ryan. Thank you for *having* Ryan. He's our hero, isn't he, Jack?" Mrs. Pedersen looks over at the bed, where Jack is lying in pretty much the same position as in the hospital, only this time he's more colorful with blue striped sheets and red pajamas. My mom's eyes get all soft and sad-looking.

"Hello, Jack," she says quietly. He turns his head but doesn't say hello. He doesn't call me his hero.

"Say hello, Jack," his mom says to him the way you would to a little kid.

"It's all right. He doesn't have to talk to me if he doesn't feel up to it. Mothers can be boring anyway. Why don't we have some coffee and leave the boys alone for a bit?" Mom puts her arm around Mrs. Pedersen's shoulder, leading her out of the room before anyone can say anything else.

I want to call them back so that I don't have to stay alone here with Jack. I want witnesses in case I get sucked in to the black hole, never to be seen again.

I want someone to tell me what to say or do to make this all better.

EIGHT

Déjà vu all over again.

The room is completely silent. I have this crazy urge to scream or sing at the top of my lungs. I don't think either choice would be too helpful.

It was my idea to come here. What the hell was I thinking?

At least Jack isn't staring at me. He's looking at the ceiling. I look up too. There's nothing much up there. White ceiling tiles. I wonder how many there are.

"So, how many tiles are there?" I ask, because I'm so talented at starting interesting conversations.

"What?" Jack turns to look at me. His eyes seem confused today instead of like dead pits of darkness. That's an improvement.

"I was just wondering if you had counted the tiles."

"Oh."

The silence comes back, heavy and prickly so that I feel like I can't breathe properly. I know the feeling is imaginary, but I still have to take a couple of quick, deep breaths to make sure. I slip my phone out of my pocket and take a quick peek at the time.

"One hundred and eighteen and a half." His voice floats out into the room, surprising me. My phone drops to the floor with a loud smashing noise. Great.

"What?" I ask, looking over the side of my chair to see if I can figure out how many pieces of phone are lying down there.

"Tiles. One hundred and eighteen and a half crappy cardboard tiles."

I stop searching for my phone and look over at him. It almost seems like he might smile.

"That's good information…I guess."

"You asked," he points out.

"That's true." I look up at the ceiling, resisting the urge to count them for myself. "Why did you come back?" he asks, taking a left turn in this pathetic excuse for a conversation.

"I'm not really sure. I just felt like I should talk to you again before…" My voice disappears into the thought.

"Before you talk to anyone else? You haven't yet?" The words come out so fast they almost trip over each other.

"Not really. The cop who was here last time said she was coming back to speak to me, but she hasn't yet. Too busy with all the crime in town, I guess. Maybe someone stole a newspaper again or something." I try a small smile, but Jack doesn't notice. We had a crime wave in town last spring when someone was stealing newspapers off people's front porches. Seeing as most people don't even buy newspapers anymore because they can read about everything on the Internet, I didn't think it was that big a deal, but it was the most dramatic thing to happen in our town in quite a while. Until last week, that is.

"Maybe. She had time to talk to me though. Wanted to know how I fell in the water." His voice cracks a little on the word *fell.*

"What did you tell her?"

"I said I was sitting on the side of the bridge where it's broken and I leaned forward to look at a duck on the water and lost my balance. I'm a shitty swimmer so when I hit the water, I panicked."

"And that's where I came in. Literally." I smile again, trying to lighten the mood. He nods but doesn't smile back.

"Yeah. You almost landed on my head." He definitely doesn't sound like he thinks I'm a hero.

"I know! I was terrified that was going to happen. That I'd kill you instead of save you." As soon as the words are out of my mouth, I want to grab them and shove them down my throat. He looks at me and his eyes go dark again. He says nothing.

"Sorry. I'm just…sorry." I shake my head.

"You're *sorry?* That you hurt yourself saving my ass? Or that you saw me dancing around in my mother's skirt? Or that you're like, the fucking hero of the century? Which one are you sorry for?" His voice is low and angry, his teeth clenched as his lips barely move.

I close my eyes for a second. I'm screwing this up. I shouldn't be here. I don't know how to deal with this. Why are the adults leaving me alone with someone who most likely just tried to drown himself in the river? Why isn't he still in the hospital so someone can fix his brain or something?

"I guess I'm sorry that any of this happened to you. I'm sorry I saw you dancing when you didn't want me to. And I don't want to be a fucking hero, but I'm not sorry I saved you because I think it would suck if you'd really drowned." I'm probably saying all the wrong shit, but no one is here to tell me different.

"It sucks more that I didn't." His voice is still low but now it sounds sad instead of angry.

"Why?" The word slips out before I have time to tell it not to. I don't want to know the answer. Not even a little bit.

Where the hell is my mother? She would know what to say.

"I just don't know how to be here anymore. I want to be somewhere else."

"Maybe you should just go on a vacation." Oh my god, I did it again. What is wrong with my mouth?

Jack looks startled and then he actually laughs for a quick second. At least I think it was a laugh. It sounded more like a bark.

"Sure. Maybe I'll go to Disneyland. That should fix everything."

"I'm sorry. Again. That was a stupid thing to say. I don't know how to talk about this. It's pretty heavy shit."

"Yeah. Well, everyone is trying to get me to talk about it, but I just keep saying that I fell in. It's no one's business but mine." He drills into me with his eyes, making sure I get the point.

"I get that."

"Good." He closes his eyes for a second. I look over at the door, hoping to see my mom coming back. I think I've said enough for today.

"I have to go back to school soon. Where everyone is talking about me, right?" His voice is just above a whisper. He's staring up at the hundred and eighteen and a half tiles again.

"Probably. I haven't been back yet because of my arm. I'm getting a new chair though, so I'll be back soon." He looks at my chair as if he'd never noticed it before.

"Shit." He whispers it, but I hear him anyway.

"It's okay. Just a pulled muscle," I lie.

"I forgot you can't even walk, and you still managed to get into the water to save me. I can't believe it. I hurt you. Everyone is going to hate me on top of everything else. Shit." He sits up and draws his knees up to his chest, hugging them tightly like he's trying to hold himself together.

"No one is going to hate you. I'm not that popular." Although Cody is pretty pissed. He can't believe I'm going to miss the swim season because of someone we barely know.

"More popular than me. Then again, Mr. St. Clair is more popular than me."

"I don't think that's true. Mr. St. Clair is pretty universally hated. My friend Cody almost took him out a couple of weeks ago. Did you hear about that?"

"No, seriously?" Jack looks interested. Anyone at our school would be interested in hearing about anything that involves personal damage to St. Clair, who loves reaming kids out and handing out week-long detentions for any little infraction.

"Totally. He slid down the main staircase railing and just missed kicking the bastard in his bald little head." I grin at the memory. St. Clair looked like he was going to puke he was so pissed. Cody landed on the floor right at the old guy's feet and just smiled at him like a big idiot. I seriously thought St. Clair was going to have a coronary.

"I never heard about that. Cody sounds…interesting."

"That's one word for him."

"Did *he* tell you that kids at school are talking about me?"

"Yeah. But you know what kids are like. They'll be all excited about this for a while and then they'll find something else."

"In this town? I doubt it. I think I'll be the conversation for a long time. What does everyone think I did?"

"I don't know what people think." He knows I'm lying.

"I don't want them to think it. It makes me a freak. *More* of a freak." He shakes his head.

"You're not a freak—any more than I am or anyone else is." I point down at my leg braces. He puts his head on his knees.

"I still can't believe you actually threw yourself into the water to save me—some weirdo dancing around in a yellow skirt. Did you even know it was me? Could you see?"

"No. I actually thought you were a girl. If I'd known you were a guy, I'd probably have just wheeled on home." I smile so he knows I'm joking. Which doesn't do much good because his head is still down.

"Would have been better," he says quietly, in that voice that makes my throat hurt.

"I don't believe that. Whatever shit is going on with you, I can't believe that." He lifts his head and stares at me.

"I don't know who I am. What I am. *Why* I am."

"Maybe someone can help you figure it out." I sure as hell can't.

"Who?"

"I don't know." A doctor? His mother? A counselor? Anyone in the world but me?

He doesn't say anything else for so long that I begin to think he's fallen asleep. That's good. He needs his rest.

"Hi, sweetie! Are you ready to go?" My mother's voice suddenly breaks in to the silence as both our moms return to the room.

"Yeah. We're good," I answer, a little too energetically. Jack kind of snorts. His mother notices and seems relieved, maybe because he's sitting up instead of lying down looking at the ceiling.

"Why is your phone in two pieces on the floor?" Mom asks, bending over to pick it up. Two pieces. Could be worse.

"I dropped it. It looks like the back just came off. I'll fix it." She hands me the phone and takes off my brakes. She wheels me over to the door, touching Jack's mom on the arm as we pass her.

"Bye, Ryan," Jack's mom says. I smile at her politely.

"Bye, Jack," my mom says.

Jack says nothing. He doesn't smile politely.

He's back to counting his one hundred and eighteen and a half ceiling tiles.

NINE

"I think you should keep this chair. It's seriously cool," Cody says as he walks beside me, making sure we're taking up the whole hallway, which means everyone is having to squeeze by while giving both of us dirty looks. This would be the only reason Cody is walking beside me. He enjoys pissing people off.

"It's big, noisy, and slower than you'd think for something that costs so much," I answer, sounding like a pissed off Eeyore watching Tigger bounce. I feel like Eeyore these days. I'm pretty sure my dad managed to find the oldest electric chair ever made. It barely moves forward, and I'm fairly certain I'm the slowest person in the school right now. I don't know why he couldn't have rented one of the high-speed, all-terrain chairs so I could at least have some fun while I can't swim. I've been back at school for three weeks now, creaking around in this geriatric chair because my stupid shoulder seems to have barely even begun to heal.

The doctor checks it every week and tells me I'm "doing fine." *Fine.* I hate that word. One of the most useless words in the dictionary. It's the typical non-answer to everyone's favorite non-question, "How are you?" Just a totally empty word that says absolutely nothing.

The first week back was strange. People I'd never even noticed before were talking to me as if we were old friends. Most of the kids at school, with the exception of Cody and my brother, were treating me like a hero, which felt awkward and kind of cool at the same time. The reporters who called were totally focused on the whole crippled kid saves a life bit, which annoyed the hell out of me. I should have had them talk to Ricky instead of me. He would have set them straight on it.

Everyone at school just wanted to know things like whether I was scared or how I hurt my arm. They asked me about the cops coming and reporters talking to me. A couple of girls even talked to me more than once, making me start to think that Ricky might be right about the positive effects of being a fake hero.

They also asked about Jack. Over and over. How he "supposedly" fell in the water. Why I thought he was there in the first place. Did I think he was trying to kill himself? Did I think he was coming back to school?

I had one answer for every Jack-related question: "I don't know."

After the first week, it got to be a little less each day. Which is good because Jack came back to school two days ago, and I'm pretty sure he's scared shitless. I would be if I were him.

I don't actually know how he feels though. I haven't talked to him at all since the second time. I couldn't think of anything else say so I just stayed away. I feel a little guilty about it but I don't know why. It's not like we're really friends.

I've seen him walking down the hall a couple of times and given him the nod. That slight tilt forward of the head that means "Hey man, I know you but not well enough to actually say anything to you." He didn't nod back—just kept on walking.

"Hey! Are you sleeping or something?" Cody steps in front of me, forcing me to release the joystick abruptly so the chair stops before I run over him.

*Joy*stick. Not exactly the right word for the controller of the most boring chair in the known universe.

"What are you doing? I almost ran over your stupid feet!"

"I've been talking to you and you're totally spaced out. So I'm trying to get your attention. Obviously." He shakes his head with a *you're-an-idiot* expression on his face.

"I didn't hear you. My chair makes too much noise."

"Whatever. Now that I have your attention, I'll ask you again. Are. You. Coming. To. Practice?" He says it slowly, one word at a time, using hand gestures to emphasize each word as if he thinks he's some kind of interpreter for the hearing impaired. Steve apparently told Cody to tell me that I should be coming to practice even though I can't swim yet. He thinks I should stick to the routine and keep track of the team's progress so I can just slip back in when I'm healed.

Steve thinks a lot of things that I try to ignore. I am not

getting up at five in the morning to *not* swim. But Cody has been bugging me to come to the after-school practices that we have. The community center with the pool in it is attached to our school so it's no big deal to go, but I haven't exactly been excited by the idea of sitting in my chair watching the other guys swim. I've been going to physio several days a week, and most of the time I manage to schedule it for swim days so that I don't think about it.

But today I actually have nothing to do.

"I guess so," I answer him in full Eeyore mode, which of course sets off Tigger again. Cody bounces about three feet in the air, raising his hand for a high five, which I can't even reach. It doesn't seem to bother him though. He just high fives the lockers and runs down the hall ahead of me.

"Get that chair in top gear. Steve'll fry our asses if you make me late," Cody yells back at me as he rounds the corner, leaving me in his dust.

This chair doesn't have a top gear. It's designed for eighty-year-olds. I can go so much faster in my own chair, and I seriously can't wait to get it back. I've been working hard in physio, but my shoulder hurts like crazy still, and it's so stiff I can't even imagine being able to wheel my chair, let alone swim, any time soon. I'm trying not to feel sorry for myself, but it's not working very well.

"Well, well. The hero has returned. Glad to see you re-membered who made you strong enough to rescue that boy in the first place." Steve is standing with his arms crossed as I come onto the pool deck. He doesn't look that happy to see me. Maybe Cody was lying about him asking to have me come back just so he could laugh at me when I did it.

"Hi, Steve." When talking to Steve, it's best to keep your sentences short and not particularly sweet.

"I assume you are planning on returning before the end of the term?" Steve asks, as if somehow I am choosing to miss practice instead of being stuck in my chair because of my shoulder.

"Yes, sir," I answer, just resisting the urge to salute with my good arm. Cody does it for me behind Steve's back, which makes me grin.

"Something funny about that?" Steve asks without turning around. Now, Cody makes a different kind of salute behind Steve's back, and I have to bite my tongue so I don't laugh.

"No, sir!" I practically shout it, which seems to startle the coach. Cody laughs and flops backwards into the water. The other guys are already in the pool warming up. Steve looks at me for a second and then turns his attention to the team, ignoring me completely for the rest of practice.

Watching people swim isn't nearly as much fun as doing it. It's hot in here and I'm literally itching to get out of my chair and into the nice cool water. I want to feel it splashing against my face as I pull myself through it, pushing my stupid shoulder out of its slump and back into shape. My whole body feels heavier than usual, held down by gravity, a sling, and an electric wheelchair.

I need to talk to my physiotherapist again about water therapy. I've been suggesting it at every session, but she thinks it's a bad idea for me because supposedly I'll push it too hard and end up with more damage than is already there. I suspect this idea came from my mother, but she won't admit it.

This is seriously annoying. I think I'd rather do homework than sit here any longer.

Cody talked me down here before I even got time to grab my books so I have to head out of the pool area and down to the connecting door between the two buildings, buzzing my chair through to the other side. The school seems completely empty. If I started to sing, I'm pretty sure my voice would echo off the lockers. If Cody was here, I'm sure he'd try it just to see. I'd rather leave it up to my imagination. I have a shitty voice. So does Cody, but that wouldn't stop him.

I wander down the deserted hall to my locker and open it to grab my books. I put them in the bag attached to my chair and check my phone. Practice will be over in a few minutes. I might as well go back and wait for Cody because I don't feel like going home yet. I don't actually want to *do* homework.

I wheel back down to the community center door and push the door opener. Nothing. I lean forward and try the handle. Still nothing. Great. The school staff has locked it from this side, so now I have to go all the way around the outside of the school.

The front door is the only one still unlocked so I head out through there and roll down the ramp, which is a hell of a lot faster in my manual chair and definitely more fun. I start to move across the pavement to the back of the school where there's an unofficial smoking area, right beside the dumpsters where the super cool kids hang out and smoke while breathing in everyone's garbage. As I move past it, keeping my distance and trying to hold my breath, I can hear voices. I don't look over at first because I'm not all that interested in knowing who is still hanging out with the garbage at this time of day instead of going somewhere more interesting and less disgusting, but the voices are so loud and obnoxious that I can't avoid hearing them.

"Seriously, you need to tell me. What the fuck were you doing?"

"Yeah, come on, you little fag. Everyone wants to know. What's the big secret?"

"Leave me alone. Please."

I've already made it past when the sound of the third voice makes me stop. I turn and look back over my shoulder.

Shit.

Jack is standing with his back up against one of the dumpsters. Two guys about twice his size are standing in front of him, obviously stopping him from leaving. I can't see who they are from this angle, but I can still hear them as I get turned around and start back over to see what's going on.

"We're not doing anything to you. We just want to know. I heard a rumor that you tried to off yourself because you're queer. Is that true?"

"Leave me alone." Jack's voice is shaking as he tries to move forward, which makes the two guys laugh. One of them pushes him back against the metal, hard enough that Jack's breath whooshes out like a deflating balloon. The guy keeps his hand on Jack's chest so he can't move.

"Just answer the question. We have the right to know if some fag is going to start hitting on us."

"Or if we're going to find you floating in the pool some day because you decide to finish the job with no crip around to save you."

"Crip. That's cool," I say quietly as I come up behind them. They turn around and stare at me, looking surprised. Obviously they can't focus on more than one thing at a time and didn't hear me coming. I recognize them, but I can't remember either of their names. They're a year ahead of us in school. A couple of local assholes who think they run the place but really just walk around acting like complete losers. The type that the gargoyles in my story would like to eat for breakfast. They're big though, so I guess that makes them think they're tough.

I'm not afraid of them. Even tough guys low on brain-power hesitate before doing anything physical to someone in a chair.

"Who the fuck are you?" The guy holding Jack turns to look at me.

"Seriously, Matt, are you a retard or what? He's obviously the crip. Look at him!" The other asshole points at my legs. Matt kind of nods. He's forgotten about Jack by now and is completely focused on me instead.

"Oh, right. The big fucking hero. Think you're special?" They're both focused on me now, and I'm hoping Jack will realize that he can get away. But he just stands there, frozen to the side of the dumpster.

"Hey, I asked you a question!" Matt yells in my face

looking like he doesn't think there's anything wrong with beating on someone in a chair.

I stare at him instead of Jack, still trying to look like I'm not afraid, but I'm not that good an actor. I'm scared shitless. This guy actually wants to pound my face in. What am I supposed to do? I can't exactly defend myself. I have one working arm and my legs only kick properly when they're in the water. Jack seems to have turned to stone, which probably doesn't make much difference because he's a little guy and likely wouldn't be much help.

"Just let us go. Okay? What do you care about some stupid rumors anyway?" I keep my voice calm and mature sounding. I'm trying to channel my mother. Coming up with wise and wonderful words to diffuse the situation. I'm pretty sure it's not working. They stare at me, unimpressed. I guess the people you're trying to diffuse would need to actually have brains for reasoning to work with them.

"We have a right to know who's going to our school. We don't have to put up with gays. Bad enough we have crips running around." Matt shakes his head in disgust at the thought of all those crips *running* around.

Obviously, words are not going to be the best weapons in my arsenal with these guys. Which doesn't leave me with much.

"Is he your boyfriend or something?" the nameless guy asks me.

"Just let us go."

"Just answer the question." He puts one hand on each arm of my chair and leans in. He's got so many craters on his face that he looks like a bad picture of the moon. His breath smells worse than the dumpsters he likes to hang out at, a nice mix of rotten food and stale cigarette smoke. Maybe I should puke in his face. That might make him back off.

I open my mouth to tell him to let us go again, but before I can get the words out, he flies backwards and spins away from me.

"Hey, Shawn, how's it hanging?" Cody says pleasantly as he shoves Craterface back against the dumpster beside Jack. Matt looks startled for a second but then lunges at Cody.

"Don't think so," Peter says, as he steps into view and grabs Matt, who starts to struggle.

"That's less than a good idea." Miguel steps up and helps Peter subdue Matt. The rest of the swim team is standing slightly behind, close enough for Matt and Craterface to realize that they're outnumbered. Assuming they can count past two.

On TV shows, it's seems to be the football team that always comes to the rescue when someone is being bullied or whatever. The quarterback makes the dramatic entrance and saves the day. No one ever thinks about the swim team. Cody is not as big as Matt and Shawn, but he swims, like, eight times a week and works out every day to build up the strength in his arms. He could hold those assholes all day and not even break a sweat.

Get the whole team together and you have a pretty unbeatable force.

I feel a new story coming on.

"You're defending gays and crips now?" Matt asks Cody.

"Nope. I'm just kicking your sorry ass. Screw off. Leave them alone. Permanently. We have their backs." Cody gestures toward the rest of the team.

"Who the hell are you guys?" Shawn asks, trying to still sound tough.

"We're the swim team, asshole. You bother either of these guys again and I'll drown you in the fucking pool," Cody says calmly, smiling at everyone as if we're at some kind of tea party in the garden instead of having a fistfight at the dumpsters.

"Yeah, well, fuck you," is Matt's well thought out and brilliant comeback as he starts to walk away.

"This isn't over," says Shawn, even though it obviously is. He follows Matt, both of them swaggering off like it was their idea.

"So, I like your new buddies," Cody says, grinning at me as if nothing significant just happened here. All the other guys start to laugh.

"Yeah, well I think you just spoiled the start of a beautiful friendship," I answer, trying to laugh too. Jack, on the other hand, looks like he's going to cry.

"Hey, Jack, I'm sorry those guys were bugging you. They're just jerks. Ignore their shit." I try to distract him. I don't think he wants to cry in front of all these guys.

"Yeah. Okay. Um…thanks."

"Ryan's right. Those guys are primo asswipes who can't actually even wipe their own asses without getting shit on their hands. Don't worry about them." Cody has such a way with words. But it makes Jack smile.

"Okay."

"They won't bug you again. Either of you." Cody looks at me and then at Jack. The rest of the guys all nod.

Who would have thought that Tigger would turn out to be an actual tiger?

TEN

It takes a while to persuade Cody and the guys that Jack and I don't need an escort home. I'm not even sure it's true. Matt and Craterface might have just gone off to get reinforcements. The whole idea that the swim team scared them away might work as a graphic novel story line, but it's likely to backfire in real life.

But I tell the guys to take off anyway. I don't want anyone to know how scared I was. How scared I still am.

How scared I'm pretty sure Jack is.

"Are you heading home?" I ask Jack, when we're finally on our own.

"No, I'm going downtown to my mom's work. She's a waitress at the Supe." The Supe is what we all call the Superior Restaurant on the main street. It's what my mother calls a greasy spoon diner because the food is so awesomely bad that it's great. Everyone from school eats there. I didn't make the connection when I saw Mrs. Pedersen at the hospital. She's probably served me about a thousand times, and I still didn't recognize her. I don't know what that says about me.

"I live in that direction. Is it okay if we head off together? Safety in numbers and all that." I try to look like I'm kidding. I'm not. If they come back, at least with two of us, maybe one will have time to call 9-1-1 while the other one keeps them busy getting beat up.

Which reminds me that I have my cell phone. It never even occurred to me to call for help when I saw those guys threatening Jack.

"I guess," Jack says less than enthusiastically as we start moving down the sidewalk.

"Sorry that shit happened to you. Those guys are jerks."

"I'm used to it. I should have just stayed away from that area. Too secluded."

"What do you mean, you're used to it? Those guys bug you before?" I've never really been threatened before. I mean, sometimes people stare at me like I have something contagious, keeping their distance as if they're afraid they'll start limping if they get too close. Other people treat me like my brain doesn't work just because my legs don't. But not too many people take the time to try to rough up a guy in a chair. Until today that is.

"Those guys. Other guys. Whoever," he says dismissively, like it's no big deal. But his eyes are saying something different.

"I didn't know. That sucks."

"Yeah, well, I'm short and skinny and not exactly athletic. My mom works in a restaurant, and my dad disappeared into the sunset. I'm a pretty easy target, I guess. And now everyone thinks I'm a suicidal nutcase, so there's that too. And the other thing." He emphasizes the last word slightly as he looks down at the ground. I wonder whether or not he wants me to admit that I know what he means or if we're supposed to talk in code.

"You mean the gay shit that they were throwing at you? Do you get called that a lot?" I finally ask, trying to keep my voice neutral.

"Sometimes. They have lots of things they call me. Gay is just one name."

"Are you?" The question comes out before I really think about it.

An image of a yellow twirling skirt flashes into my mind, making me feel like I really want to be somewhere else talking about something...anything...else.

"Does it matter?" He stops walking, still looking down at the pavement. I roll to a stop also.

"Not to me. Some people around here think there's something weird about it. Maybe most. This town isn't exactly full of rainbows." He searches my face as if he's trying to read something written on it. I'm not sure what he's looking for but I guess he finds it because he starts talking again.

"No. Not exactly. I think I might be the only gay guy in the entire town." He closes his eyes quickly as if he's afraid to see my reaction this time. He's standing so still that it seems like he's holding his breath, just waiting for me to say or do something.

I wonder if it's the first time he's said it out loud.

I wonder what I'm supposed to say or do.

"I doubt it but you can't be sure, I guess. I don't actually *know* of anyone else. But I don't know everyone in town. I don't even know everyone in our grade at school." I keep my tone casual, cool even. Like it's no big deal.

"You don't know what it's like being the only one," he says slowly, as if the words are being pulled out of his mouth one at a time. His eyes are open now but he's staring at his shoes again instead of looking at me.

"I kind of do," I say back, pointing down at my legs. "I'm pretty sure I'm the only person under the age of like, ninety, who uses a chair in this town. Seems bizarre but I guess it's a really small town. Lots of one-offs." His eyes shift from his shoes to mine.

"I never thought of that. But it's not really the same, is it? No one thinks there's something wrong with you. I mean, something *bad* about you, like you're going to infect them with something."

"That does happen a little. Some people seem afraid of me, like they'll catch whatever I have and forget how to walk or something. I've been called a crip by losers a few times. But I guess it isn't the same." No one ever acts like they hate me or want to hurt me because of who I am. Except for those idiots today, and I'm pretty sure they do that to everyone.

"You wouldn't believe how many people around here use *gay* as an insult. *Fag, queer*…whatever label they can find that makes it a bad thing to be. Not even directed at me most of the time. Just at anyone they're trying to piss off. I can't imagine what it would be like if anyone found out that I actually *am* what some of them call me." He shudders a bit.

I think about it for a second. I want to tell him he's wrong, but I can't. Most of the guys I know use those exact insults. They think it's funny most of the time.

Do I call other guys *gay* or a *fag* when I'm trying to insult them? I don't even know. Cody does it all the time. Probably most of the swim team does.

I don't want to imagine what it would be like if anyone found out Jack really *is* gay.

"Well, they won't hear it from me. I stay out of other people's business."

"Really?" His voice is totally sarcastic, and it takes me a second to understand what he's saying.

"Well, most of the time. Except when I'm trying to be a hero." I try grinning humbly.

"Yeah. Except that. Remind me to thank you some day. Do you remember where you hid my…stuff?" He takes a quick turn in the conversation and I have to think a second before I answer.

"Not exactly. It's under a bush somewhere. I'm pretty sure it's a green one, if that helps." He smiles, just a little.

"Probably not much. I guess I'll have to try to find it. My mom will eventually notice her skirt is gone."

"Yeah, my mom is always super pissed when I go swimming in her clothes and then leave them at the beach." I instantly want to bite my tongue in two. That was *so* not funny.

Jack lets out a full laugh, surprising me into joining him.

He starts walking again without warning, and it takes me a few seconds to get my chair going so I can keep up.

"You're pretty weird, you know," he says to me as I come up behind him. He slows his pace until I'm beside him again.

"Yeah, I know."

"I'm weirder."

"That's probably a matter of opinion."

"Most people in this town would think a guy…a *gay* guy…who likes to dress up is weird." The twirling skirt flies into my view again and I have to agree with him.

"Maybe. There are probably people, outside in the real world, who would be cool with it though."

"Yeah, well that doesn't help me any. I can't get out of this place. I'm stuck here forever." His voice cracks a little.

"That's not true. We only have this year and next left in school. Then you can go away. Get a job or go to college, whatever you want." That's my plan. I want to find somewhere to live where I'm not the only one on wheels. Where all the buildings are living in the twenty-first century so that they're actually accessible.

"It's not that easy. My family is…complicated. And I just made everything worse."

"By *falling* into the river?"

"Yeah, right. They know I'm lying. Even though I'm sticking to my story. They still know. My mother's probably freaking out right now because I'm late getting to the restaurant. She probably already called the cops. She's so scared it'll happen again."

"Will it?" Everything goes quiet as the words hang suspended in the air between us. I really wish I could reach up and grab them, putting them back inside my stupid brain where they belong.

I seriously need to know when to shut up because *A*: he's not going to tell me the truth about something like that and *B*: I don't *want* to know the truth about something like that.

We're both quiet for so long that I start hoping he isn't going to answer.

"I don't know. I screwed everything up royally this time." The words come out just above a whisper. He stops walking again and just stands there. I release the joystick on my chair and sit looking at him. He's staring straight ahead, and I'm not even sure he knows I'm still here.

I don't know how to talk to someone about the how *not* to screw up drowning himself so this time I keep my mouth shut. I should do that permanently. Silence is probably a good thing.

"I wish I could morph into a caterpillar." The words come out of nowhere, and I react without thinking.

"Why the hell would you want to be an insect?" So much for keeping my mouth shut. Maybe I should just keep on moving and leave the guy alone on the sidewalk.

He looks at me for a second before smiling slightly, looking embarrassed.

"A caterpillar is basically gross and ugly. But then it gets to hang out in a cocoon for a while and ends up changing into a gorgeous butterfly. Beautiful colors all floating on the breeze, dancing around wherever it wants to go. No one cares if it's a boy or a girl. It's just a caterpillar that changed into a butterfly. And it's okay and right and normal." He shrugs his shoulders as his eyes fill up with tears, and one escapes and sneaks down his cheek.

My own eyes sting a little, which is ridiculous because I do not cry. Ever. It's a waste of energy. My mother cries enough for everyone in our house. She calls it cathartic. I call it tears and snot all mixing together in a gross mess.

"I looked it up by the way. Some people say they can and others say they can't."

"What?" He looks at me, confused.

"Swim. Caterpillars. You asked me when I saw you at the hospital if I thought they could swim so I looked it up on the Internet and didn't really find a clear answer. Some sites say they can if they have to, and others say they just drown."

"Oh. Thanks, I guess."

Now I'm embarrassed. I'm not even sure why I looked it up in the first place.

He starts walking again, and I move along beside him.

"Anyway, I'm turning here. Thank your friends for helping. I didn't want to get beat up. I don't really like pain much." Jack's smile seems both artificial and sad.

"I don't think anyone does. Especially not pain from crater-faced assholes who think they're tough." My smile feels as fake as Jack's looks.

"Yeah. Anyway, I guess I'll see you around school." He turns to walk to the restaurant.

"Yeah, definitely. Listen, Jack, let me give you my cell

number. Just in case you need me for anything. Or Cody and his swim gang," I say, trying to sound casual and cool about it all. He turns and then gets out his phone.

"Okay. I guess. Shit, I was right. Eight missed calls. All my mom." He shakes his head as I give him my number and he logs it in. I expect him to give me his number as well, but he just puts his phone away and walks down toward the Supe.

I head home. My mother is probably still at her work, too, so she won't be wondering where I was after school. I'm sure not going to tell her about Matt and Craterface. She'll get me a babysitter.

Apparently I already have one. Cody the hero. Never would have guessed it in a million years. I know he's strong but he's always seemed like the passive type...in a hyperactive, mildly insane kind of way.

I don't know if those guys will leave us alone just because the guys told them to. My mother always tells Ricky and me that bullies are cowards and will back down if confronted most of the time. It sounds logical, but from what I've seen and heard, confronting guys like Matt usually results in a broken nose.

I hope no one on the team ends up hurt because of me. It's bad enough that I screwed them over by having to sit out half of the term. I don't need to make it all worse by trying to be a superhero every five minutes.

I think I liked my life better when the only thing I was known for was sitting in a chair and hanging out with the swim team.

ELEVEN

"Hey." I answer my phone on the first ring, hoping for an escape from doing homework.

"Hi. Am I interrupting anything?"

"No. I'm just thinking about doing some homework."

"Oh." Jack goes silent for a few seconds, and I start to wonder if he's disappeared.

"Are you still there?"

"Yeah, sorry. My mom was just talking to me. I guess you're busy."

"Not really. Math can wait."

"I was just wondering if I could come over for a bit. My mother is working a double, and I'm stuck in the restaurant for another three hours. It's Thursday."

For some reason, Thursday has always been the night that kids from our school like to go down to the Supe and sit eating fries all night. Obviously not Jack's favorite time to be stuck there.

"Sure. You can help me with my math. I seriously suck at it."

"I'm probably not much better, but I can try."

I am nowhere close to convinced that the whole Shawn/Matt saga is over, even though Cody is totally sure that they'll never bug us again. So over the past couple of weeks, I've been trying to make sure that Jack doesn't end up anywhere alone, which means I'm spending time with him that I hadn't planned on. It's mostly all right though, as long as I don't let myself think about what he was doing that day at the river. He hasn't said anything depressing recently, and I don't really mind hanging around with him. At least he's pretty quiet, which is a contrast to Cody.

Jack arrives a few minutes after his call. Mom meets him at the door and lets him in. She's always extremely nice to him, but I get the feeling that she isn't particularly thrilled with my spending time with him. She seemed pleased with the first couple of visits, as if she was proud of me for being a nice guy or something, but recently she seems to be uncomfortable around him. No, that's wrong. She seems to be uncomfortable with the idea of me being around him. Which is weird because my mom's basically the tolerance champion of the universe.

"Hey," he says as he comes into my room. He comes over to the desk and pulls some books out of his bag.

"Hi."

"Is it okay if I use this chair?" he asks, gesturing to my desk chair. I look at him, a bit surprised that he'd ask.

I don't really need a desk chair, but I get sick of being in a wheelchair all the time so I like to transfer if I'm going to be working for a while. For today, I'm sitting at the end of the desk in my manual chair because I'm so excited to have it back that I might never get out of it again. I finally have the stupid sling gone off of my arm and have been working on getting enough strength back to actually move with something resembling speed again.

"Yeah, go ahead."

"Are you sure? I mean, if you would be more comfortable in it, I can just work on the bed or grab a chair from the kitchen or something." If Cody was here instead of Jack, he'd already be sitting there with his feet up on the desk. He doesn't pay a lot of attention to anyone but himself most of the time. Except for pretty girls and brainless jerks who need an ass-kicking.

If he had been the one on the bridge that day, he probably wouldn't have even noticed Jack was in the water.

Maybe I should be more like Cody.

"No, I'm okay. I want to spend as much time in my wheelchair as I can to get my shoulder working again. Even just moving around my room helps it. Thanks, though."

He nods and starts working. The room is silent for a while as we both try to focus on the boredom that is homework. After a few minutes he looks up.

"I was at the clinic today."

"Oh. Are you sick or something?"

"No. At least not the way you mean, I guess. My mom makes me go see this counselor guy named Charles, who's trying to get inside my head. Because of what happened." He shrugs a little, looking as uncomfortable as I'm starting to feel. I don't think this is going to be about math.

"At the river?" I ask, even though I know that's what he means. "Yeah. He wants me to admit that I was trying to…hurt myself. That it wasn't an accident." His voice is low, hesitant, as if the words are having trouble finding their way out of his mouth. I wish they'd stop trying. I really just want to go back to silent math. I don't want to talk about this.

"Did you? Admit it, I mean?" I ask him. He looks at me quickly, eyes all wet and red. He sniffs loudly and rubs both hands over his face, scrubbing like he's trying to wash something away. He's quiet again for so long that I think maybe the conversation is over and I'm off the hook.

"No. I don't even know if there's anything to admit. It *was* kind of an accident." He hunches up his shoulders, both palms facing the ceiling as if he's wondering if it's going to start leaking.

"What do you mean?" *He accidentally walked into the water with his mother's skirt on?*

He sits back a little. "I don't know how to explain it. I don't even know if you want me to."

No! I don't. Let's just do math or talk about TV or play a video game. Something normal.

"Sure. If you want to. I mean, I can listen. I don't think I can help much." I shrug, and my bum shoulder actually manages to move without screaming at me. Progress.

"I snuck out of the house early that day, before anyone else in town would be around. At least I thought no one else would be around." He looks at me, and I try an encouraging nod.

"Anyway, I took my mother's skirt because I just wanted to see how it would feel. How *I* would feel."

He stops talking and closes his eyes. Is he imagining himself twirling around again in the flowers? If he is, that makes two of us.

"You're the only one who knows that I'm…gay. For real that is. I mean, there are rumors at school. I don't know how they got started…"

"It wasn't me."

"I know. I think that out of all the different ideas people had about me, that one stuck. Partly because of how I look." He stares at me for a second. I don't know exactly what looking gay means but I guess Jack doesn't look like a football player. Like he said before, he's short and pretty thin. He has curly hair that he wears kind of longer than most guys around here. But other than that, I don't see that he looks all that different from anyone else.

"You look normal to me."

"Thanks."

"Shit. I said that wrong. I just mean, you look like anyone else at school. I don't know what there is about you that looks gay or anything else." I'm tripping over my tongue here. Why did I say he could talk to me? I suck at this.

Cody never talks about anything but swimming, skateboards, or girls.

"If I dressed the way I wanted to, everyone would definitely know!"

81

"The skirt."

"Yeah. I like skirts and dresses. Always have. And jewelry. Makeup. Not every day or anything, but it's just…fun to dress up sometimes. It feels…I don't know…nice. Sometimes I try my mom's stuff on when I'm sure no one is going to catch me. I like the way it looks on me. I like how I feel when I'm wearing it." His cheeks are turning bright red.

"Okay. That's your business, right?"

"Right! My life. My business. Except…" He shakes his head and closes his eyes.

"Except what?"

"Except I can't actually live my life. Not here. I can't put on a dress and makeup and head down to the Supe. I don't think anyone would be cool with that. Your swim-team friends would likely help Matt kick the shit out of me if they saw me like that."

I want to tell him that he's wrong. That people would eventually accept him whatever he decided to wear or put on his face. That no one would care if he fell in love with a guy or a girl. But I'd be lying if I did.

"Are you a transvestite? Or a transsexual?" There's a lot about equal rights on TV and the Internet these days. The city where my CP doctors are has a Pride Parade every year. There's even a town near here that has one now. I think our town is a few years away from anything like that.

"No. I don't think so. I don't want to be a girl. And I don't need to wear dresses all the time or anything. I just wish I could when I wanted to, you know? And fall in love with whoever I want to. I don't know why I need to label myself. I'm just me.

But apparently that isn't enough, and I don't understand why."

He seems shocked that all those words spewed out of his mouth. He looks at me, wide-eyed and obviously expecting me to say something.

I'm trying to find an opinion. I'm not sure that I've ever thought about this before.

A guy in a dress *would* be big deal around here and probably a lot of other places. I know this is true but I realize in this exact moment that I don't know why, either.

"I guess it's just different," I say lamely.

"Yeah, well different can get you hurt." He's right about that, but I don't bother agreeing out loud.

"Do your parents know?"

"No!" The word shoots out into the room, startling us both. He shakes his head a little. "I can never tell them I'm gay. My mother's über-religious and my dad thinks that real men play football and kill things. He's like every stereotype on TV of the intolerant man's man who thinks he's right about everything. He'd likely decide never to talk to me again if he knew…which might not make much difference to me because I've barely seen him since the divorce anyway. But my mother would cry for three weeks straight if she found out and try to take me to church so I could get fixed."

I think about Jack's mom sitting endlessly by the window in his hospital room, her eyes so tired that they couldn't stay open.

"Your mom really loves you." He looks at me for a second and then nods slowly.

"That makes it all so much worse. She would be heart-broken if she knew so I have to hide it forever. My mom does everything for me. She's the best. I can't stand the thought of hurting her. I'd rather…" His voice trails off as he puts a hand over his eyes. He sits like that for a long time.

"I'm so tired of having to pretend to be someone else. I'm so tired of being…ashamed of wanting to be myself. I'm so tired of being scared someone will find out. So tired." His voice disappears on the last word.

I don't have any idea what I'm supposed to say to him. I can't think of a single word that would make it better.

We sit there quietly for a few seconds. Eventually Jack speaks.

"So, I went to the water that day to see how it would feel. Just to be…me, you know? Just for a few minutes. And at first, it felt great. Dancing, spinning. The fabric twirling around me like I was some kind of diva dancing on a grand stage. I felt like I could *do* anything. *Be* anything. I felt like I wanted to just stay there forever where no one would call me names and I wouldn't have to tell anyone who I am and deal with them hating me or making fun of me. Or not *wanting* me anymore."

He takes a deep breath and exhales slowly.

"I couldn't stay at the water's edge all day dancing because people were going to come and see me and then they'd know. Everyone would *know*. So I had to go home and put my mom's skirt back and go to school like I do every other day. Pretend to be whoever everyone else thinks I am…like every day."

"Did you see me on the bridge? Is that why…?"

"No! No, I didn't see you. I only saw the water. It looked so calm and quiet. Safe somehow. I could imagine how it would feel to just walk in and let it kind of wrap around me. Just let everything disappear—float away. It seemed like it would feel so nice. Make life better for a while."

His eyes are closed, remembering.

"I walked in and the water felt nice and cool, like I could breathe better than on dry land. So I kept going, one step at a time, just feeling everything drift away as I got in deeper and deeper. It started to seem like the pain was actually going to disappear forever if I could keep going. I just wanted to keep going until I couldn't feel anymore." He smiles slightly for a second, shaking his head. "And then it all went to hell. It was like I had been dragged under a giant wet blanket and I couldn't breathe. My heart felt like it was going to burst and my lungs felt like they were going to explode and turn my ribs into sawdust. I couldn't find my arms and legs. Everything was black and painful. It was horrible. And then there was this big splash right before I blacked out, which I realized later was you almost landing on my head." He folds his arms, hugging himself.

"You see? I can't tell the counselor I was trying to hurt myself on purpose because I wasn't. I was trying to make the hurting stop."

TWELVE

"So, Jack is looking a little better today," Mom says to me as I enter the kitchen after Jack has left.

I didn't know listening to someone could make me need sugar the same way swim practice makes me need carbs. Lots of sugar.

Except that my mother is standing in front of me so I reach for an apple instead of raiding the cupboard for cookies.

"Is he? I didn't really notice."

"I think you've been good for him. He seems…lighter somehow." *Lighter?* She obviously didn't see him leave after what was probably the heaviest conversation I've ever had in my life.

"I don't think that's because of me. He goes to a counselor every week." I say it like it's some sort of obvious fact instead of something I just found out myself.

"I know that. His mother told me when I called her to see how she's doing. But I still think he values his friendship with you. I just want you to be…careful."

I chew the mouthful of apple I just bit off and look at her, trying to figure out what she means. Did someone tell her about the dumpsters?

"Careful of what exactly?" I ask, swallowing before I talk so she doesn't start a lecture about manners.

She pauses for a few seconds and then breathes out a sigh.

"It's just that…well, I am proud of you. For saving Jack that day and for trying to be his friend afterwards. I wouldn't have wanted you to do anything differently. It's just…I'm worried about Jack and the severity of his issues, and I'm not sure that he can handle a new friendship right now."

"That doesn't even make sense. How do you *handle* a friendship?" What does that even mean? What is she talking about?

"I'm not explaining this well. I'm trying to say that my responsibility…my concern…is for you. Of course I want the best for Jack, and I desperately hope that he finds his way through this time with his body and soul intact. But I also want the best for you. And being friends with someone as…troubled as he is might not be in your best interest."

I have my apple heading toward my mouth for another bite, but her words stop it halfway there. Seriously, *what* is she talking about? My mother has spent my whole life lecturing me about being kind to others. Being tolerant and understanding. Accepting everyone for who they are. Not being judgmental. Being loyal and respectful. The list goes on.

And suddenly I'm supposed to ditch someone because he hates his life?

"It doesn't hurt me to hang out with Jack." It makes me uncomfortable sometimes, sure. It scares the shit out of me occasionally too. But I'm not going to tell her that.

"Does he talk to you about that day?"

"He talks about lots of stuff." Why is she asking me about this today? Was she listening outside the door? Ricky and I have always had a theory that our mother is a serial eavesdropper. Either that or freakishly psychic.

Either way, Jack's personal life is none of my mother's business. He has his own mom. And his own counselor.

And I guess now he has me, too.

Oh, and of course he has Cody to keep his shit from being kicked out of him.

"Well, if he ever says anything to you that makes you uncomfortable or upset, please tell me." She's looking at me intently, trying to reach in there and read my mind. Mom radar. I hate that.

"Sure. Whatever. He's not dangerous or anything, you know. He's just screwed up, like most kids." My voice sounds whiney and defensive, which I'm sure is really helping here.

"Most kids don't end up in the river."

"*I* did."

She smiles and ruffles my hair.

"I know. And *you* know that's different. You're quite a guy, you know that? I love you. Just…take care of yourself. Okay?" She bends down and gives me a kiss on the forehead and heads out of the room. I look down at my apple, which is still halfway to my mouth. It doesn't look the least bit appetizing.

I head over to the cupboards, which are all low enough for me to reach, compliments of one of my dad's DIY projects. I have to dig through three of them before I find the cookie stash. I think Ricky hides them so he can have them all to himself. I grab a bag and put it beside my leg and head back to my room so I can shove some sugar down my throat and try to do some work so I don't get in shit tomorrow during class. The novelty of my hero status wore off with my teachers about three seconds after I came back to school, and no one seemed too interested in any excuses I came up with for falling behind in my classes.

The cookies give me a sugar high that lasts just long enough to get my work done before I come crashing down to earth. It's only ten, but I'm so tired I can't keep my eyes open so I head into my bathroom to get organized before coming out and shifting onto my bed. I sit on the edge and take my braces off, massaging each leg and foot so I can relax enough to get myself to sleep. My legs tend to work in opposition to the rest of me. When I'm really tired, they like to spring into action, tightening up and pulling my muscles into weird shapes until the cramping is so bad I can't even think about sleeping. If I'm careful, I can launch a pre-emptive strike, using techniques my physio taught me to loosen them up and force them into some kind of submission so I can rest.

I'm tired, but my brain feels wired, wound so tight there's no way I'm going to fall asleep even if my legs behave themselves.

I wonder if Jack is right about how his parents would react if he told them the truth.

I've never really thought about any of this shit before. I've heard about it, I guess. I mean, I've heard guys on those reality talent shows tell stories about how their parents kicked them out because they're gay or whatever. I never thought much about it though. They were just stories that happened to other people.

I'm thinking about it now—thanks to Jack. Thinking about how hard it is to be different from what people want you to be.

I'm sure I'm different from what my parents wanted me to be. I don't think they wished for a kid who couldn't walk. But they've never made me feel that they would want me any other way—that they're disappointed in how I turned out.

My mother told me she's proud of me. She tells me that a lot. She also tells me that I should take pride in myself. My accomplishments. Even my "disability."

We had all of these talks at the rehab center about how having a disability, being *different,* shouldn't be seen as some big problem in your life. That you have to own it instead of fight it.

Like the X-Men. *Mutant and proud.*

I'm not exactly proud of the fact that I can't walk. But I'm not ashamed or embarrassed either. It's just me.

To be honest, my neon hair embarrasses me more than my chair ever could. It's just *me* too, but I still think I'm going to dye it when I move away some day.

I know most people are surprised, even amazed, when they find out I'm on the high school swim team with guys who can walk. I am proud to be on the team. But I think everyone who made it feels that way. I'm not sure I feel any better about it than they do just because I roll into the water instead of dive.

There's this expression I've heard that goes something like, "you can't miss something you never had." Which I assume would imply that I can't miss walking because I've never been able to do it, and therefore I'm completely cool with the way things are.

The expression isn't true. At least not for me. Or maybe it just needs to be changed a little. I think you can miss something you *wish* you had. I *wish* I could walk. It's not that I sit around feeling sorry for myself all the time. It's just that sometimes I feel like I'm missing out because I live in a chair.

For example, girls might look at me differently than they do now if I was standing up instead of sitting down.

Some girls stare at my chair instead of my face when they meet me. Other girls try so hard to pretend it isn't there that it turns into the mysterious, invisible wheelchair that apparently only I can see. Then, just to make it interesting, still others act like they're doing their community service hours every time they see me, trying to help me instead of trying to get to know me.

It's hard not to wonder what it would be like to have a girl just look at *me,* without my wheelchair blurring her vision.

Maybe someday that will change and I'll end up in a place where I'm so proud of myself that I don't want anything to be different—like Cody. He actually thinks he's perfect. Although, he might be alone in that opinion.

I don't know. Maybe I'm just using the word wrong.

Proud. Filled with pride.

Pride. Like the parade. The one that Jack would probably like to march in if he ever got the chance.

He's not proud of being gay. He's just plain terrified.

I can't imagine what it would feel like to think your dad could hate you and your mother could be hurt and disappointed in you because of who you are. Or who you want to be.

People seriously suck sometimes.

Gay pride.

Disability pride.

Maybe we should just have *being-a-decent-human-being* pride.

THIRTEEN

"So, are we still going or what?" Cody says, pulling himself up onto the side of the pool.

I push my goggles up on my forehead and rub my shoulder. Once he realized I was back in my own chair and able to make it move, Cody decided it was time to get me into the pool. After my mom got the go-ahead from the doctor, Cody appointed himself my private swim tutor, so whenever he isn't busy, he's making me work. He's not as bitchy as Steve, but he definitely pushes me just as hard in his own way. I'm starting to think he has a career as a swim coach in his future. He has this way of getting me to keep pushing without making it seem like he's doing anything at all. He just calmly says things like, "Guess you don't really need to be on the fall team. You can always wait until winter," which of course makes me want to prove him wrong every time, even though I know that he's just playing mind games.

"What are you talking about?" I didn't hear him talking about anything. I'm concentrating on trying to remember how to swim.

"Comic Con. This summer. Us. Remember? We talked about it? Like a million times?"

"I know we've talked about Comic Con a million times, but I don't remember actually deciding to go to one. When is it and where is it?"

"It's in July and it's in Bainesville. You know this! We talked about this last fall and decided that it will never be closer to us, so we're going to go. I can't believe you forgot! I already have my costume ready. Man, save some loser kid's life and you forget all about the important shit." He shakes his head hard enough to spray me.

"He's not some loser kid, Cody."

"No, he's just some whack job who tried to off himself a few weeks ago and could do it again but this time finish what he started." He rubs the water out of his eyes and looks at me.

"In the first place, you don't know anything about what he was or wasn't trying to do and in the second place, it's more than a few weeks now and he's doing fine." Whatever that means.

"Still don't know why you spend so much time with the guy. He's not exactly your *type*." He grins when he says the last word, wiggling his eyebrows up and down like a dirty-minded clown.

"You're just hilarious. He's a *friend*, Cody. Like you."

"He's nothing like me. I'm an original and much cooler than him or any of your other so-called friends. You can stop procrastinating now and get moving. We'll make our Comic

Con plans later when you're thinking straight. Get it? Thinking *straight?*" He laughs at his own stupid joke as he shoves me off the side of the pool without warning, making me swallow a nice mouthful of chlorine as I head down. I come up sputtering and choking.

"Screw off, Cody!" I shout at him between coughing fits.

"Happy to!" he shouts back and takes off down the pool, strong and fast and making me feel like shit because I'm so ridiculously slow still. This sucks on so many levels I can't even dive down to find them.

I take a couple of seconds to get my breathing under control as I rotate my shoulder a few times. It's moving without creaking these days even though it's throbbing like crazy, but I'm not going to tell Cody that and listen to him laugh. I take off down the pool after him, trying to focus on my form instead of the discomfort.

"That was actually better. Pissing you off seems to work. I'll have to remember that," Cody says to me as I struggle out of the water and roll onto the deck. I lie on my back, panting up at the ceiling.

"Remind me to drown you next time we come here," I say to him when I catch enough breath to talk.

"Sure. If you can catch me, you can give it your best shot. You ready to go again?" He jumps up and looks down at me with a big shit-eating smile on his face.

I stare up at him and shake my head. He shakes his hair so that the water splashes down into my eyes.

"Am I annoying you yet?"

"You've been annoying me since the day we met. And you can piss me off all you want, I'm not getting back in there until I feel like it."

"Wimp!" He runs to the edge of the pool and throws himself in, sprinting to the other end before I can even get myself sitting up.

Cody's right about one thing. He is an original. I remember the day I met him. Grade five. We had just moved to the new house, and I had to switch schools. I was not happy about it. I didn't want to get used to a new school. I didn't want to try to figure out how to navigate a new set of hallways and find out whether I could use the bathrooms or not. I didn't want to have to get a new set of teachers used to me. Most of all, I didn't want to have to get a new set of kids used to me. I'd been at my other school since kindergarten, and the kids there had basically grown up with me. No one stared at my chair or at me when I shifted out of it to sit down on the floor. I had friends there who hung with me at recess even though I couldn't join the soccer games or go up into the field to make fun of the girls.

My parents had to take me to the new school before I started so that the teachers could figure out how to make sure everything was going to work for me there. I had to practice wheeling up and down the aisles in my classroom so that they were sure the desks were far enough apart. We had to talk about what to do in a fire drill to make sure I got out okay. We had to figure out the doors and make sure I could get in and out on my own. At least this school wasn't built before the last century so it had an accessible bathroom, but I still had to practice to make sure I could get in through the door on my own so we would know if I would need what the teacher there called a "helper."

I hate helpers. I know by definition that they're just trying to help but in my experience they fall into two categories: volunteer helpers, who are obnoxiously nice about the whole thing because they think they're doing something special, and forced helpers, who would rather do anything else than push some crippled kid around. Either way, it's usually awkward. I'd rather figure it out on my own or have someone who is actually a friend help me when I need it.

Cody was a forced helper. It was the very first day of school and I was sitting in the classroom waiting for a black hole to open up and swallow me so I didn't have to feel any more stares burning into my back from the kids in my new class. For some reason, my teacher felt that having a practice fire drill on the first day of school would be a wonderful idea. She had decided in our interview the week before that one student would be "assigned" the terribly exciting job of making sure I got out of the classroom safely.

She was explaining all the fire safety rules and the proper behavior that she expected from her class and all that crap. Everyone was pretending to listen except this one kid. He was staring out the window, making hand gestures at someone outside. He was so into his sign language conversation that he actually jumped up out of his seat and went over to the window.

"Cody McNeely! Sit down right now!"

The kid doesn't even slow down. He keeps sending hand signals out the window for at least another thirty seconds while smoke starts coming out of the teacher's ears. Maybe that fire drill won't be a practice after all.

"Cody!" She screams it, and he finally stops and turns around. He has a big grin on his face. He looks straight at me and winks.

"Sorry, Mrs. Smithson," he says in a super sweet, totally sarcastic voice.

"*Miss* Smithson, as you well know. Cody, I think you can be Ryan's helper for fire drills." She nods as if she's done something good.

It's always nice to be used as a punishment for someone else on the first day of school.

Cody just laughs and sits down.

"Cool," he says, as he salutes. I'm not sure if the salute is for me or Miss Smithson. It doesn't matter. The whole class is trying not to giggle. They're also probably taking note of the fact that they'd better behave or they'll be stuck helping the kid in the chair.

"Okay, the fire signal has started. Let's move!" Miss Smithson sings out, and everyone gets up and lines up. Cody comes over to me and starts trying to push my chair.

"Shit man, you're heavier than you look!" he says.

I reach over and release the brakes. The chair shoots forward, because he's still pushing full force, and I smash into the wall. The footrests take most of the impact, but I can still feel the jarring all the way up to my head.

"Oops. Screwed that one up!" Cody says cheerfully. He manages to get me spun away from the wall and out the door.

The rest of the class is out of sight by the time we manage to even get into the hallway.

"Fast little buggers, aren't they? If this was real we'd be both be roasting by now! Guess we'd better get moving!" He starts running down the hall, pushing me from side to side until I start to feel my breakfast trying to make an appearance in my mouth. He gets me to the door and shoves me out onto the front step. There's a small ramp there, but he either doesn't see it or chooses to ignore it because he just bumps me down the three cement steps onto the parking lot. My teeth smash together and I'm pretty sure I can taste blood as I try to bite my tongue in half.

"Almost there!" he shouts as he takes off again, aiming for the rest of the class, who are lined up neatly on the other side of the yard, watching us coming at them. I'm pretty sure the blood is dripping down my face by now. I know the sweat is.

Cody finally stops moving when we arrive at the end of the line.

"Ta-dah!" he says, as Miss Smithson covers her face with her hands and all the kids start to laugh.

The good thing about it is they aren't laughing at me. They're laughing at Cody. I was just along for the ride. Literally.

I sit there for a second with my wet face and sore teeth, watching Cody take a few bows and then I start to laugh too. I laugh until a few tears and some snot join the mess on my face. Miss Smithson shakes her head.

"Oh, I'm Cody by the way," Cody says to me, which seems like the funniest thing anyone has ever said to me in the history of everything and makes me laugh even harder.

And that was it. We've been friends since that moment.

Cody doesn't seem to really care that I'm in a chair. He's never asked me if my legs hurt or are paralyzed or any of the other questions I'm used to being asked by kids. He never cuts me any slack in swim practice. He bugs me just as much as he does everyone else. He makes fun of me when I try to talk to girls and laughs at my hair on pretty much a daily basis. He calls me a bunch of names that I don't like to repeat and tries to get me to do his homework. He doesn't talk to me about personal stuff. I have trouble imagining him having any personal stuff. And I never talk to him about anything that I wouldn't want repeated to anyone who happened to be walking by. Cody isn't exactly the world's expert on keeping secrets, which I found out the one time I made the mistake of telling him that I thought a girl in our class was cute.

"Are you seriously still lying there?" Cody has swum back to my end of the pool and is leaning with both elbows out of the water on the edge looking at me.

"I am seriously still lying here. Very seriously," I answer… seriously.

"Well, you are seriously lazy and even more seriously out of shape. And now the word seriously is starting to sound seriously stupid because we've said it too many times. Seriously."

"Will you shut up if I get in the frigging water?"

"I will if you're serious."

"I am seriously going to roll on your head and hold you under until you turn blue."

"Yeah, well you'd have to get off your fat ass and catch me

first. So bring it." He pushes himself off, backwards into the water, backstroking his way across the pool. I roll over and up onto my knees, moving as quickly as I can over to the edge and launch in after him, laughing a little as I try to catch up.

I think my swim grin is coming back.

FOURTEEN

"Gargoyles who come to life at night and wreak revenge on high school assholes?" Jack laughs.

"Well, it sounds better inside my head. And will be even better once I get it written down properly. I hope." Now that I'm saying it out loud, my formerly awesome graphic novel story line is sounding relatively lame.

"So, have you started it yet?" Jack's trying to seem interested but is obviously wondering why the hell I'm babbling about story ideas.

Mostly I was running out of things to talk about, and I'm just trying to keep the conversation on topics inside my comfort zone.

"Just barely. I can write pretty well now that my shoulder has healed enough that I can use both hands. But I can't draw worth shit."

"I can draw pretty well. I get decent marks in art even though it drives me nuts having to do what the art teacher says instead of my own thing."

"I noticed some sketches you drew in your math book. You actually draw really well."

"Thanks, but that wasn't exactly my best stuff."

"Well, it looked good to me. I thought maybe you'd be interested in helping me with my novel."

"That kind of drawing isn't exactly my favorite thing to do, but I guess I could try. I'm just not sure how good I'd be." He doesn't sound very enthusiastic.

"I think you'd be great, but if you're really not into it, that's fine. It was just an idea. What *is* your favorite thing to do?" Jack doesn't answer for so long that I start to get that uncomfortable feeling again, the one where I'm afraid he's going to start talking about personal things. He has been avoiding talking about any of the crap going on in his life recently. I've been kind of relieved, hoping that maybe he's sharing with someone else…someone who can respond with some kind of intelligence.

"You don't have to tell me if it's private or whatever," I say to him when the silence starts to stretch out and his eyes start to get darker.

"No. It's not a big deal. It's just something else that I can't do."

"Oh. Well, I probably can't actually write a graphic novel that anyone will give a shit about either."

"I don't know. Your story sounds bizarre enough to work."

"Thanks. I think." He smiles for a quick second and his eyes start to come back to normal.

"I guess I'll tell you. It's really no big thing. It's just that I have always really wanted to be a singer. I even took lessons for a while when I was younger, until my dad said they were a stupid waste of time and too expensive…even though we had enough money for him to make me play soccer, which I hated. Anyway, I've always dreamt of being on a big stage, with cool costumes and lots of crazy makeup that I could actually wear without anyone thinking it's weird." He looks embarrassed.

"If you want to be a singer, why not go for it?"

"I'm pretty sure my parents want me to get a real job… right here where I can help out at home. When my dad left, he told me I had to take care of my mom." His eyes close and he puts his head back against a tree. We're sitting down by the river. Jack likes to go there for reasons that I don't really want to think about. I'm able to get over the bridge on my own steam again and then he helps push me the rest of the way over the rougher ground to the grass and trees at the top of the hill. We can sit and look at the exact spot where all the drama happened without being in the way of anyone trying to use the bridge. He never talks about it when we're here but the thought of it is always hovering in the back of my mind, buzzing around like a fly that needs to be swatted. I'm always slightly afraid that he'll suddenly start running and end up back in the water before I can do anything about it.

"Well, maybe you should enter one of those singing shows and win lots of money so you can be a singer, impress your parents, and get the hell out of town all at the same time."

"Sure. And maybe in this alternate happy universe of yours, I can admit I'm gay too, and no one at school will kick the shit out of me, and we'll all live happily ever after."

His eyes are still closed. His whole face looks closed. We're definitely heading into the danger zone.

"Anyway, it's getting late and my mom will be complaining that I haven't done my homework if I don't get moving." It's lame, but I can't think of anything else. My stomach is starting to dance around a bit, and I really think we need to get away from here.

He sits there completely still for just long enough that the dancing turns to buzzing, as if the flies have migrated from my head to my gut.

"Yeah, okay. I guess I should check in with my mom, too." He finally opens his eyes as he gets up to help me move over the grass until I'm on pavement and can wheel myself easily across the bridge. He slips back into silence as I mentally kick myself for starting him down into his black hole again.

I guess mentally is the only way I *can* kick myself. Ha-ha. *Shut up, Ryan.*

I should say something to him. I don't want him going off by himself feeling upset. But I don't know what to say. This sucks.

"Um, so, do you want to come to Comic Con with me this summer?"

He looks at me as if I just asked him to go for a swim in the river.

"What?"

"Comic Con. It's like a big festival thing where everyone dresses up and semi-famous people sign autographs…"

"I know what it is. I have a TV and a computer. I'm just not sure why you're asking me."

He's not the only one. I didn't think this one through. Cody is going to throw a complete shit fit if Jack actually says yes.

"It's this summer in Bainesville, which is only a few hours away from here. I've always wanted to go to one, and it might be fun for you too. Even if you're not into graphic novel stuff, it would be a chance to, I don't know, get away from here for a while. Out into the real world."

"You want me to go to a fantasy comic book festival so that I can experience the real world." Sarcasm drips from each word as he shakes his head at me. I just laugh…mostly at myself because he does have a point.

"Bainesville is a hell of a lot bigger than here, and there'll be people there from all over the place, and everyone is totally weird so no one thinks anyone else is weird. You get to go in costume if you want. You can be whoever you want to be for one whole day." I'm making this up as I go along and probably digging myself a really nice deep hole to fall into.

Jack looks directly at me, his eyes seeming interested for a second before they go dark again. He shakes his head.

"I don't know. My mom is pretty much stalking me still. I'm not sure she'd be cool with me going away overnight."

"Well, it's not until late July, so maybe she'd be okay with it by then." Or maybe she'll never be okay with it, and then I won't have to deal with the wrath of Cody.

"Sure. Whatever. I'll think about it. See you later," he says, looking less than thrilled with my brilliant suggestion as he turns away from me and heads down toward the restaurant.

As I watch him walk for a bit, I get the distinct feeling that I didn't manage to make anything better. I think I somehow made it worse.

I can't think of anything else to do, so I just head for home. When I get there, Cody is on the front porch, using my ramp for skateboard tricks. I get a sudden pain right in the middle of my forehead as I imagine having to tell him what I just did.

"Check it out!" he yells at me as I come up the driveway. He flies down the ramp and tries to jump off his board and spin around. At least I think that's what he's trying to do, but I can't be sure because he mostly just flies up into the air and comes crashing down onto the driveway, grinning in front of me.

"Guess I need a bit more practice."

"Steve will fry your ass if you hurt yourself. It's bad enough that I'm just starting to get my shoulder back into shape. He can't afford to lose you too."

"I'm tougher than that. It'll take more than a skateboard to take me out! Besides, you'll be back soon. I timed you yesterday. You're getting faster."

"Yeah, so fast I can almost make it down the whole pool without stopping more than three times to rest. I don't think I'll be back to full competition level until next term, maybe not even then." I'm so pissed with my body these days. Even though my shoulder is obviously healing, my swimming is still nowhere close to being as strong or as fast as it needs to be yet.

"Sucks to be you. You aren't pissed at Jack for doing this to you? You seem to spend a lot of time with someone who totally screwed up your year."

He has a good point. But I don't really think about it that way. I mean, Jack didn't ask me to fling myself dramatically into the water.

I still wish it didn't happen.

Mostly, I wish Jack's life didn't suck so much that he ended up in the river in the first place.

"I don't spend that much time with him. And it will be even less now that I'm going to be starting back to practices for the rest of the month. It's been pretty boring this term without anything much to do after school. Hanging with Jack's been better than nothing." On the other hand, hanging with Jack *and* Cody at Comic Con might definitely be worse than nothing.

The hole is getting deeper by the second.

"Okay. Whatever you say. Anyway, I don't have anything to do right now, so you can hang with me. I'm bored."

"Lucky me. So, what do you want to do?"

"I don't know. You can watch me practice my skateboarding while we talk about the trip."

"That sounds like fun."

Cody nods cheerfully, missing the sarcasm. "It will be. You get to critique my style. You can channel big Steve and bitch me out while we figure out how to get you a decent costume."

He heads back up the ramp to set up the next death defying challenge. I shake my head at him but can't help grinning at the same time.

I think I'll wait a while before telling him that I invited Jack.

FIFTEEN

"So, I've been thinking about your idea." Jack's sitting on the edge of the bridge, swinging his legs over the water while I try to *not* imagine him rolling forward and into the river.

I keep telling Cody to stop thinking about what Jack did and just let him get on with his life. I obviously need to tell myself the same thing.

"Yeah?" It's been more than a week since I first mentioned it to him. I was actually hoping he'd forgotten all about it.

Cody's getting more excited every day, even though he doesn't like my costume. He's going as Captain America because he thinks it fits his personality. I kind of thought he should go as Tigger, which would likely be a total original, but he shoved me backwards into the swimming pool and threatened to sit on my head when I suggested it. Cody thinks I should go as Xavier, which is what everyone would expect me to do, which is exactly why I'm not going to do it. I thought Cody had more imagina-tion than that. Anyway, he is not impressed with my Wolverine costume, which I ordered online and is totally kickass.

He would be even less impressed with my bringing Jack along. To put it mildly.

"It kind of sounds like it could be okay." Jack's looking down at his swinging feet.

"Don't get too enthusiastic or anything," I say, laughing. He shrugs and smiles a little.

"Yeah, well, it's pretty complicated but I came up with kind of a plan that I've been trying."

"What's that?"

"Well, my counselor hasn't been very thrilled with my progress because I don't actually like to talk to him because I haven't had anything to say."

"Must be pretty quiet."

"Very. Mostly we've just been sitting there while he waits for me to open up or whatever he calls it. Anyway, in my last session I started talking…just a little. Telling him shit like how hard the divorce has been on me and crap like that. I thought if he figured I was actually making what he thinks is progress, admitting I've been having problems, he might help me get my mom onside for the trip. It's just one night, right?"

"Well, it depends on a couple of things we're still trying to figure out, but probably just one."

"What kinds of things?"

"Well, transportation for one thing. Accommodation for the other."

"Wouldn't we just we take the bus?" he asks.

"I don't think *we* can. At least not around here. We found that out the hard way when my mom and I needed to go to the city one time when our car wasn't working. My mother was so pissed I thought she was going to pound on the bus driver because he wouldn't let me on!"

"He actually wouldn't let you on?" He looks at me surprised.

"Nope. I had a ticket and everything. But he told us the long distance buses around here don't have lifts so they're only accessible if you can walk well enough to get yourself up the stairs. He said that the ticket agent shouldn't have sold me a ticket without checking first and that I couldn't just randomly get on a bus that wasn't equipped for people *like me*. That any bus driver had the right to refuse to let me on if he was worried about how I would get off in an emergency or whatever."

"Man, that sucks. It's weird, I don't really think about what being in the chair means for you. Maybe because we basically met when you were busy saving my life. I don't know. But I just never thought about the shit you have to deal with." He seems concerned that he did something wrong.

"Don't worry about it. I'm used to it. For stuff like this, it just means that I have to do a bit more planning than other people do. No big deal."

I still remember the look on my mother's face when they turned us away. It seemed like a big deal to her. Her face was red and her eyes were full of tears. She actually clenched her fists when she was talking to the driver, and I thought she might swing one in his direction.

The rule on the buses around here is that they'll transport your scooter or chair as luggage so long as you're mobile enough to get yourself onto the bus. So, basically, I'm not welcome.

I don't want to travel on their smelly instruments of travel torture anyway. Trains are better. At least the ones I've been on are. They have wheelchair accessible cars and special entrance ramps and lifts, depending on the particular train. The people there help you on and off and treat you like a human. The only problem is that there aren't nearly as many trains as buses, plus the nearest train station is almost an hour away. So unless the bus system changes, I'll have to get my license and drive myself everywhere if I want to be completely independent. Which means I'll have to have my own car. Silver lining.

I'm pretty sure for this trip the plan was for Cody to drive us in his older brother's car. Don't think that would be a selling point with Jack, so I'll hold on to it for now.

Jack's sitting quietly while I go on a mind tour. He's probably having one of his own, trying to figure out if a weekend at Comic Con is worth the effort.

"Anyway, I'm still figuring out the transportation stuff, but I'll take care of that part and let you know."

"And you said the other thing was accommodation?"

"Right. I think I have that figured out. I have a friend in Bainesville. Well, not exactly a friend. A guy I met in the hospital rehab center there a few years ago when I was recovering from one of my surgeries."

"*One* of your surgeries?"

"Yeah, I've had a few." I look down at my legs.

"What kind?"

"Different things. All related to my CP."

"CP?"

"Cerebral Palsy. It's what makes my legs like this. There're a lot of different types, and pretty much everyone who has it is affected in their own way. I mostly have problems from the knees down, although I've had some hip problems too, and also a few seizures when I was younger."

"Shit." He looks surprised.

"Yeah, it's mostly shit. But lots of kids are worse off than me so I guess it's all relative. Anyway, I had surgery on my legs a few times. My muscles and tendons stiffen up and cause bad cramping. My feet are all twisted up, and my ankles are screwed up too. The surgeries were to try to ease some stress. When I was really little, I think they were hoping that I could be helped enough to be able to walk, but that was a no go." I shrug my shoulders. "Anyway, I met Jacob when I was in rehab, like I was saying. He's older than us, by like three years or so, but he's cool. We've kept in touch a bit, and I asked him if we could stay there. He said his parents wouldn't mind, so we have that option."

"My mom might actually be okay with something like that, especially if my counselor tells her he's making me all *better.*" He puts a sarcastic spin on the last word.

"Sounds good to me. In the meantime, you should do some research and figure out a costume. I'm doing Wolverine." No comment. Either Jack doesn't think it's weird for Wolverine to be in a chair or he doesn't actually know who Wolverine is.

"Yeah, I'll really have to think about that part. I don't really read a lot of comics but I've seen a few movies. I used to dream I was a superhero." He says the last part quickly, looking a little embarrassed.

"Seriously? Which one?"

"Just one I made up. *Jay the Great.* Original, I know! I used to fly around saving the lives of kids in my school. No one ever recognized me even though I don't think I had much of a disguise. I wore turquoise spandex with a hot pink cape, sort of like Superman with a makeover, which no one thought was weird because everyone loved me in dreamland. I even dreamt that the school burned down one night and I saved the asshole in my class who loved to make my life shit during the day but didn't know me when I flew him safely out of the inferno at night. I can still see him blubbering, snot all dripping down his face while he thanked me."

"Sounds intense."

"I was eight. It all seemed cool to me. Anyway, I don't think I'll come as Jay the Great." He laughs a little.

"Well, you need to give yourself time to order something or make it if you know how to do that kind of stuff. Do you have any money?" I didn't think about that part before. His mom's a waitress and his dad's living somewhere else. Maybe he can't afford to come.

"Some. I bus tables sometimes at the restaurant and I get to keep what I make so I can buy stuff my mom can't afford. I think I have enough if I decide to come."

"Okay. Well, I hope you do. It'll be fun!" My voice is too

loud and enthusiastic, like a cheerleader hyped up on energy drinks. He looks a bit startled and then gets up.

"I have to head to the restaurant now."

"Yeah, I have to motor too. Cody is likely waiting at the pool by now."

Cody.

Shit.

I still haven't told either of them that there could be three of us on this road trip.

SIXTEEN

"You did *what?*" Cody looks at me like he wishes we were still in the pool so he could drown me. I decided to wait until after we finished practice and were safely on dry land. Just in case.

Obviously a good call.

"I invited Jack to Comic Con." I repeat it even though he obviously heard me the first time.

"Why…*why* would you do that? What the hell is wrong with you? I don't want some little gay drowning victim nut case screwing up my weekend. Shit. Seriously, Ryan, you act like you're in love with the guy or something." He's pacing up and down the ramp in front of the community center, stomping his feet like a three-year-old having a temper tantrum.

"Now you're just saying stupid shit."

"No, you're the one saying stupid shit. Inviting that guy on our trip is seriously, seriously stupid shit!" He smacks his hand on the railing so hard that he hurts himself.

"Fuck!" He yells as he grabs his hand and presses it against his chest, wincing.

"Can you just calm down for two seconds and let me explain?" I need to think fast because I don't really have a reasonable explanation. What do I tell him? That I was feeling sorry for Jack one day because his eyes were turning into black holes, so I invited him to Comic Con without asking Cody first? It even sounds pathetic inside my own head.

Cody looks at me with murder pretty clearly written in both eyes, shaking his head and his sore hand at the same time.

"I'm perfectly calm. I've never been calmer. See how calm I am? Just go ahead and explain why you want to wreck our one chance to go to Comic Con." He stretches his mouth across his face in a really creepy imitation of a smile. I'm glad I'm at the bottom of the ramp instead of the top where he could give me a friendly push to help me down.

I take a deep breath, praying to whatever gods might be out there that I can find something to say that will sound remotely reasonable to the fire-breathing version of Cody.

"Jack's not a bad guy. He's just dealing with some crap in his life. I've been trying to be a friend to him, I guess. Mostly because I've had the time but partly because he's okay to hang around with, too. He doesn't have many friends, and I just thought it would be nice for him to get a chance to get out of this place for a bit after all that happened."

"*All that happened*…meaning he tried to drown himself and you had to risk your life saving his sorry ass!" Cody looks even angrier, if that's possible.

"I didn't risk my life. I just helped him, that's all." What is *he* so pissed about?

"You *just* helped him. You live in a fucking wheelchair. You threw yourself into the water, screwed up your shoulder, and still had to swim with the guy and get him to shore. You seriously don't get that you *both* could have died?" His eyes are shooting sparks.

"I'm a strong swimmer. Just like you. You would have done the same thing if you'd been there."

He closes his eyes for a few seconds and does a few deep breathing exercises. When he looks at me again, he doesn't seem quite as pissed, but then he doesn't seem quite ready for a happy dance either.

"I don't think I would have done anything. Maybe called 9-1-1. I don't think I would have thrown myself in the river for some stranger." He's shaking his head.

"I don't believe that at all. You're the strongest swimmer in the school. You've got your life saving certificate. Shit, you work as a lifeguard in the summer at the pool. I know you would have saved him."

"Nice that you think so. I'm not so sure. And I know that even if I *had* saved him, I wouldn't have decided I had to be his friend, too. The guy's like a pariah at school. Everyone knows he's gay. It's not exactly helping your cool factor to be hanging with him."

"In the first place, no one *knows* anything about him." *Except me.* "And in the second place, I don't give a shit about anyone's opinion. I know I'm cool." I try a grin in his general direction. He just scowls at me.

"So, is he actually gay or what?"

"Why are you even asking me that? I just told you no one knows. Why does it even matter?"

"Everyone says it. I also heard that he's depressed. And I think someone said he's schizoid. Oh, and I heard that he's been doing heavy drugs."

"Sounds like you know everything you need to. And then some." I don't know why everyone doesn't just get over it already.

"Come on, Ryan. Everyone is still wondering why he tried to kill himself, and I think that you're the only one who's got the inside track, so you need to give up some answers. That's fair."

"No one even knows for sure that's what he was doing. What's fair is leaving the guy the hell alone!" The words slap at him and he looks at me, surprised.

"Hey, don't bitch me out. I don't spread the rumors. I just listen to them. Besides, if I left the guy alone, he'd have had the shit kicked out of him. Or did you forget?" He holds up his uninjured fist and shadow boxes the air in front of my face.

"No, great hero of the masses. I did not forget. Hopefully Matt and Craterface didn't either."

"Craterface? Oh, you mean Shawn. That's awesome! A much better name for him. I think I'll use it next time I see him."

"That'll help you keep the peace." I shake my head at him. He just laughs.

"Have they bugged you again? Or Jack?"

"Not yet."

"They won't. They're scared of the Code Man."

"*Code* Man?"

"Yeah, me!" He points at his chest, then gives himself a thumbs up. I wonder what it would be like to love yourself that much.

"Yeah, I got that. So, is your super power creating codes or breaking them?" He looks at me like I just started speaking Spanish…a subject Cody failed two years in a row because he forgot to go to most of the classes.

"What the hell are you talking about?"

"Nothing. Anyway, *Code Man*, you have to decide if we're going together or not."

"You never answered me about Jack."

"Does the answer matter?"

"I don't know. I don't know any gay guys. At least I don't think I do. Unless your spending all that time with Jack means something you want to share…?" He smiles and raises his eyebrows.

"Screw off."

"Gay guy in a wheelchair. Two strikes!" He laughs and tries to high-five me but I keep my hands down.

Gay guy in a wheelchair. Would that be two strikes?

I guess I only have one strike in Cody's world. I like girls. A lot. My problem is that I don't know how to talk to them. When I try to talk to a girl, my tongue gets as messed up as my legs, as if it's tied up in plastic braces and can't move properly.

Of course, I could never talk to Cody about it. He wouldn't get it. He's tall, athletic, funny, and easygoing. He's never had any problems finding female company.

"You are such an asshole," I tell him. He stares at me for a couple of seconds and then smiles, shaking his head.

"You are such a jerk, Ryan. Seriously. I can't believe we have to bring a gay kid to Comic Con. He's not going to hit on me, is he?"

"You don't know that he's gay. And even if he is, I'm sure he could resist you."

"I don't know. I'm pretty sexy," he says, grinning full on.

"So, you're okay with this?"

"Nope. Not even close. But I want to go. And I want to go with you because we planned it whether you actually remember that or not, so I guess your little buddy can come along if he has to. We'll just stay away from large bodies of water, and I'll try to tone down my sex appeal. Good enough?"

"Good enough. Sort of. Anyway, we'll talk about the rest of it later." I start wheeling my way into the house.

"The rest of it? What do you mean, the *rest* of it?" His voice trails after me as I make my getaway. I don't want to talk about Jacob in this exact moment. I'm pretty sure Cody had plans for a motel. I'm also pretty sure that Jack's mother wouldn't be thrilled with that plan. Mine either.

But I'll save that whole conversation for another day.

Now, while I'm on a roll…so to speak…I'm going to find Jack and tell him. This day is just going to keep getting better and better.

I find him at the restaurant, just ending a shift, and decide to tell him ripping-off-the-bandage style—just a quick tug followed by a stinging sensation and then it's all over.

"No way!" He looks at me like I'm totally crazy. Which is probably fair.

"Sorry, I should have told you before. The whole trip was actually his idea in the first place."

"Cody. For a whole weekend. Does he know you invited *me?*"

"Yeah, and he's cool with it." I'm hoping he can't hear the lie.

"I don't know." He shakes his head. "I mean, I appreciate that he's been protecting us and everything, but other than that Cody isn't much different from any of the other guys around here. It's going to feel like we never left Thompson Mills."

"I really want you to come, and since it's basically Cody's trip, not to mention the fact that he's also our ride, he has to come too. He won't do anything stupid. It will be fine." There's that word again.

"He's our *ride!* Are you serious? The guy is totally hyper. I finally managed to persuade my mother that nothing bad is going to happen if she lets me go. You're sure he isn't going to drive us into a tree?" Jack's eyes are wide and worried.

"He's actually a better driver than you'd think. He's had his license for almost a year and so far hasn't cracked up any cars or people…that I know of." Cody's a year older than Jack and me, due to some "issues" in elementary school that had him repeating a grade, and he got his license in the first possible second that he was old enough. He lives on a farm and has been driving the family's old truck around the property since he was about twelve. As long as he remembers we're on a road and not cruising down the back forty, we should be fine. I hope.

"Oh, well that's good. I feel a *lot* better now." He's obviously not convinced.

"It's going to be fine. Better than that. It will be fun. A whole weekend away from here with our own ride and some independence for a change." Even though I'm likely going to be playing referee the whole weekend.

Jack takes a deep breath.

"I'm probably going to regret this but I guess I'll come. Now that my mother said yes, I don't really want to go backwards and tell her I'm not going. That would probably give her something new to worry about. She likes to worry. Which makes me a good son for her, I guess."

"All mothers like to worry. It's in the job description. My mother took almost as much persuading as yours did." Once my mom knew that Jack was coming along, she wasn't exactly jumping over the moon. But my powers of persuasion are legendary.

Of course, I also heard my father telling her that it's time for her to loosen the umbilical cord a little and let me grow up. Mom's not the only serial eavesdropper in the house. Ricky and I have perfected the art of finding places where we can overhear our parents' conversations.

"I guess. My mom does a really good job of it." Jack rolls his eyes.

"Have you got your costume ready yet?"

"Not exactly. Working on it."

"Well, let me know if you need any help."

"Thanks. I'll be fine. Anyway, I have to go. Talk to you later." He doesn't look exactly excited.

Shit. This is going to be nuts. I don't want to go on a trip with these two guys. I started all this by accident.

So why am I trying to persuade everyone that this is the greatest idea of the century?

SEVENTEEN

The rest of the school year crawled along at its usual breakneck speed, making it seem like summer was never going to come.

Not that summer is as exciting as it used to be when we were younger. Cody and Jack have both been working pretty much full-time since classes ended, so right now I'm not seeing much of either of them. I was supposed to try to get a job this year, too, but my mom took pity on me and said I should spend the time getting better and working on my swimming instead. I wasn't sure what I was going to be able to find in town anyway. I can't exactly clear tables at the Supe, like Jack. The aisles in that place are narrow, and I'd be knocking waitresses over left and right.

Most of the stores in town have the same kids who come back year after year, and there are seldom any new job options. And if there were, I'd probably not be their first choice. There isn't exactly stellar accessibility in our town yet, except in the bigger chain stores out on the highway, which isn't close enough to get to without help. I suppose if I really took the time to go in and talk to a few managers, I'd find someone willing to try to figure out something for me, but for this summer, I'm happy with the reprieve.

My shoulder feels more like it's slogging through mud than slicing through the water, so even though I managed to get back in to a couple of team practices before the year ended, I mostly worked by myself off to one side while Steve gave me the stink eye from the other side of the pool. I'm trying not to panic, trying to believe Cody when he says that I'm improving. I know I have to be patient, that if I work it the wrong way, I'll just make things worse and I won't even get back on the team full-time by fall.

Assuming I'm still around in the fall. First I have to survive a road trip with two guys who want to be anywhere but with each other.

Jack's level of enthusiasm for the trip didn't exactly increase with time, but he didn't back out either. Which is good, I guess.

Cody has finally stopped bitching about Jack coming with us, but he apparently has strong opinions about the rest of my plan.

"No way! I already booked us a motel."

"I didn't know you were going to do that. I've already talked to Jacob and he's expecting us."

"His *parents* are expecting us you mean."

"Well, yeah, they'll be there too. It's their house. Jacob is a good guy. You'll like him." I don't know if that's true or not. I haven't actually seen him in years.

"I'm sure your friend is very nice and everything, but this is *our* trip. We didn't plan on parental supervision when we talked about it last fall. It's enough that your friend Jackie baby is coming. I'm not giving up the rest of the trip just because his mommy doesn't think he's old enough for a motel." He looks at me, disgusted. I've been doing laps while he finished up his lifeguarding shift, and we're sitting on the edge of the pool while I catch my breath.

"It isn't just his mom. Mine was worried about where we were going to stay, too, and only calmed down when I told her about Jacob." She more than calmed down. She was pretty close to thrilled that I'd be safely in someone's house with his parents standing guard.

"This is stupid. You're seventeen now. I'm turning eighteen soon. We're freaking old enough to go away on our own for a couple of days." I shift over a little, trying to keep out of easy pushing range. I'm not ready for another dip just yet.

"I know that. You know that. But my mother doesn't. If you want me to come, then we have to have my mom onside."

Cody has both fists clenched like he wants to punch something. He sits like that for a few seconds and then suddenly jumps to his feet, teetering a bit on the edge of the pool until I think he's going to fall in. He catches his balance and smiles.

"I have an idea!"

That's never good. Cody's ideas haven't historically been the kind that end well.

"We say we're going to your friend's place but we really go to the motel. No one has to know. Not even Jack, so that he doesn't have to actually lie to his mommy. We can tell him your friend got sick or something last minute and we had to find somewhere different to stay."

"So, I'd be the only one lying to my mom?" *And to Jack.*

He looks at me, considering.

"Well, no. I might as well lie too. Keep the stories straight just in case. Anyway, they'll never find out. We'll be keeping in contact through our cell phones so they wouldn't have any idea where we're staying."

"Knowing my mom, she has a tracking program."

"Your mom isn't that paranoid. Is she?"

"No, probably not." I hope.

"Okay, then. Compromise. We say we're going to your friend's place but we go to the Shady Rest Motel with a six-pack that I stole from my brother instead."

I think Cody needs to look up the definition of *compromise.* This seems more like a capitulation.

"The *Shady Rest* Motel?"

"The finest motel Bainesville has to offer."

"Seriously?"

"No. It's the only motel anywhere close that has any rooms left because it's Comic Con weekend and the city only has two hotels. It's about ten minutes outside of the city, but it's better than nothing. And definitely better than going to someone's house where we have to make nice for his parents." He nods at himself, looking pleased with his own logic.

I'm not sure about that. I was kind of looking forward to seeing Jacob. I met him after one of my surgeries back when I was twelve or thirteen. The rehab center had a program where older kids acted as mentors to younger ones. They helped with the actual exercises but also talked to us, gave advice, whatever worked. Jacob was one of the most popular volunteers. He was cool and funny. He made fun of the staff, held wheelchair races in the hallways, and told awesomely rude jokes that would have made my mother faint in horror. I actually think Cody would really like him.

I only got to work with him for a few weeks, but we kept in touch a little bit online afterwards. I haven't seen him live and in person since then, so it would be really nice to go to his place.

My mother was really happy with the idea that I was going to see him again. All she remembers about Jacob is that he was a mature, responsible volunteer in a wheelchair who helped me through a tough time. She'd be hoping that he would give me equally mature, responsible advice about life as a young adult in a chair.

Cody is splashing his feet in the water cheerfully, probably because he figures he's won the argument. Which I guess he has. After all, he's already given in on Jack coming with us. I can't push this any further without royally pissing him off again.

Looks like I'm not going to be seeing Jacob any time soon.

"Okay," I tell Cody, even though I'm pretty sure it's not.

I think Jack might pass out at the idea of The Shady Rest Motel and a six-pack. Cody might be right about keeping it from him until the last possible minute.

Three weeks of lying to Jack. Not to mention my mother. Definitely a capitulation. I'm so screwed.

EIGHTEEN

"Ready?"

Cody bounces out of his brother's car and runs up the ramp to where I'm sitting waiting on the front porch. It's eight o'clock in the morning and we're getting ready to head off to Bainesville.

Somehow I got through the three weeks without saying the wrong thing to anyone. It's pretty close to a miracle.

The next miracle will be surviving the next two days. I've already been on the phone with Jack twice this morning, persuading him that everything is going to be okay.

Now, who's going to persuade me?

"I guess so. Just let me tell my mom we're heading out." She's been fussing around me all morning, making sure I have everything, checking my phone to make sure it's working so she can call me every five minutes. Basically treating me like

I'm seven instead of just turned seventeen. You'd think I was the first kid in the history of time who actually went away for a weekend without his mommy and daddy.

She finally lets me back out the door, then stands in the living room window watching me transfer into the front seat of the car. She has a Kleenex pressed up against her face, which means the waterworks are starting again. I don't know if she's crying this time because she's worried or because I'm so grown up or because her favorite rosebush died.

I don't know what she'd be doing right now if she really knew the truth about our trip. She definitely thinks we're staying with Jacob for the night, fully supervised by his parents. I'm not sure what she'd do if she knew that Cody talked me into going to a motel.

Cody manages to fold my wheelchair and shoves it into the back of the SUV. He turns and waves cheerfully at my mother, who puts a brave smile on, waving back before she turns away, wiping at her eyes.

"Your mom's crying," Cody says as he settles in to his seat and starts the car.

"Yeah, she cries a lot."

"Probably tears of joy because she's getting rid of you for a whole weekend." He grins as he backs out onto the road. "My mom didn't cry. She did a happy dance."

"I'm not surprised. I only have to put up with you for one weekend. She has you all the time."

"Ha-ha. You'd better be careful what you say to me. I have your life in my hands." He takes both hands off the steering wheel and waves them in the air. He'd better not do that with Jack in the car.

"Yeah, well try not to kill me in the first thirty seconds," I say, reaching over to grab the steering wheel myself as he bats me away and puts his hands back where they should be.

"Keep your hands to yourself! If you want to drive, get your license."

"Easy for you to say. I can do the written but I'm not sure how to practice driving. My dad's car doesn't have hand controls."

"I never thought of that. What're you supposed to do then?"

"I'm not exactly sure. I can't afford to retrofit a car. You can buy portable controls but I'd still need someone to teach me how to use them, I think. I don't know. My parents aren't all that interested in me driving so we haven't talked about it much. I've been trying to do some research so I guess I'll start bugging them about it once I know what I'm talking about."

"So basically never, because you *never* know what you're talking about."

"You're so funny I might actually laugh."

"Yeah, well, you'd be the only one then. That guy looks like he's going to a funeral." Cody points over toward where Jack is standing at the end of his driveway.

He's holding his backpack in front of him like a shield and is staring down the road at us. Cody's right. He does look like someone just died.

Not the right thought for the beginning of our trip.

We pull up in front of him and I roll down my window as Cody stops the car.

"Hey!" Cody barely smothers a laugh as Jack looks at me like a deer about to be run over by an SUV.

"Hi," he says.

"So, hop in!" *Hop* in? First he's a deer, now he's a rabbit.

Jack gets into the back seat. He does not hop. It's more like inching his way across the seat, as if he can't believe he's actually doing this.

"Hi Jack," Cody says, looking at him in the rearview mirror.

"Hi." The word is barely audible. I glance at Jack over my shoulder. He's staring out the side window, obviously not interested in a chat, so I turn back.

Cody rolls his eyes as he puts the car in gear.

I can pretty much hear his thought. It's the same as mine. *This is going to be so much fun.*

The car is freakishly quiet for the first while. Even Cody seems to have forgotten how to talk, although that's probably a good thing because it hopefully means he's concentrating on remembering how to get there. It's only about a three hour drive so we'll be there by noon. We're registered for the afternoon sessions today and the full day tomorrow. We're heading straight for the festival, which is good because it delays the time when I have to tell Jack our plans for the night have "changed."

He's still staring out the side window, probably wondering how I persuaded him to come on this super fun trip in the first place.

"So, Jack, are you actually gay or what?" Cody asks suddenly, smashing the silence into a thousand pieces.

"Cody!" I punch him on the arm, just enough for him to feel it but hopefully not hard enough to make him swerve into the other lane. I look over my shoulder. Jack has pulled his eyes away from the passing wheat fields and is staring at Cody's back.

"Ow. Don't hit me. I'm driving here," Cody says, trying to sound wounded but obviously enjoying himself. Jack is still quietly staring.

I'm searching my mind, trying to find something remotely intelligent to say that might diffuse the situation but there's nothing in there that'll help. Better to just shut up.

The silence fills the car until it takes the air away and I have to open the window so that I can breathe. The lovely smell of cow shit in the summer wafts in.

"That stinks. Close the window. I'll put the AC on," Cody says, wrinkling up his nose.

"You live on a farm."

"Yeah, exactly. I literally have to deal with that shit every day. I'm trying to get away from all that."

"Me too." The voice comes quietly from the back seat, shutting both of us up for a second.

"What?" asks Cody.

"I'm trying to get away from the shit I deal with every day too." Jack's voice is soft, but I can hear the anger vibrating through it.

"You mean, like cow shit?" Cody says as I shake my head at him.

"No, I mean like *your* shit. And everyone else who won't stop asking me if I'm gay or on drugs or trying to kill myself or anything else they can come up with to make it impossible for me to walk down the hall at school without wanting to hide in a locker."

Cody looks at him in the rearview mirror for a second. I'd rather he looked at the road.

"I wasn't trying to give you any shit, man. I was just asking. Trying to get to know you or whatever."

"Really? You couldn't think of anything more interesting to ask me about?"

I should be interrupting here, trying to start a better conversation so that the trip doesn't end before we even get there.

"I don't think Cody meant anything…" I start, but Cody interrupts my interruption.

"Thanks, but I don't need help talking. It's cool. I wasn't trying to piss you off, Jack. I was just…I don't know…curious."

"Well, think of something else to be curious about. I don't want to talk about *that.*"

Cody obviously can't think of anything else to be curious about because the car gets quiet again. The AC is blowing nice cool air in my face and Jack has gone back to staring out the window. Cody is focusing on the road.

"It should be just up here," Cody says after what feels like at least six hours instead of three. We left the wheat fields behind a while back and have been passing strip malls and fast food restaurants as we enter the city limits. The golden arches are making my stomach complain, and I'm wondering if I should suggest we stop and grab lunch.

"Good. We're almost there," I tell Jack redundantly. He's only three feet away so he probably heard Cody.

"Okay," he answers, looking at me for the first time since we left home. I try a nice encouraging smile. He just shrugs his shoulders. He doesn't look hungry. Maybe I'll just forget about lunch for now.

Cody navigates us through a few streets and then we pull up to a large arena. There are cars and people everywhere. Cody sits for a minute, trying to figure out where we're supposed to go. The car behind us honks impatiently, and Cody offers the driver a polite suggestion with his middle finger. He pulls forward, looping around in front of the building and back out onto the main road.

"There has to be a sign or something telling us where the hell to park."

"Over there to the left," Jack says from the back, pointing toward a giant sign that we somehow missed on the first pass. Cody heads toward it slowly, trying to figure out exactly where he's supposed to be.

We get into a lineup of other cars doing the same thing. There are people floating around with neon orange vests on, presumably directing traffic but mostly just walking around trying to look important. I keep waiting for Cody to make some comment about my hair and how I wouldn't even need a vest or whatever, but he's concentrating too hard on trying to follow the crowd to remember to bug me. Everything that seems like a regular parking space looks full, and we just keep driving farther and farther away from the arena.

Finally, one of the pseudo traffic cops waves at us dramatically, pointing to a spot on the grass that doesn't look big enough for a motorcycle, let alone our car. Cody swears to himself as he carefully squeezes in and stops.

"Did it," he says proudly, looking over at me. I nod.

"Yeah, except for one thing."

"What?"

"I can't get out of the car." I point to the car beside us, which is about half an arm's length away.

"You can just squeeze…oh, shit. Right. Your wheelchair." He looks behind him. "I'll have to wait until there's a big enough gap so I can back up and get you out. Could be a while."

We sit for a few minutes until the stream of cars has been redirected to the next lot and then Cody backs the car out far enough that we can get my door fully open. He stops again and heads back to get my chair. Jack gets out of the back and comes over to me.

"Can I help?" he asks.

"No, that's okay. Cody's used to it," I tell him as Cody wheels the chair over and parks it beside the open door.

"Brakes," I say to him.

"Right. Forgot." He puts the brakes on and holds the handles on the back to give a bit of extra stability on the grass. I brace one hand on the chair as I slide my butt across the car seat, easing myself toward the door. Cody's car seat is higher than my dad's so it's not a straight across transfer. I have to go across and then get down without falling or destroying my shoulder again.

It takes longer than usual, but I get myself down and in. Cody pulls me clear of the door and slams it shut, then pulls my chair back so I can get turned around.

"Okay. Let's go." I start trying to wheel across the grass and manage to get stuck in about ten seconds.

"Here. I'll push you until we get onto the pavement," Cody says, stepping toward the back of my chair. Jack moves forward, getting there before him.

"No, I'll do it," he says. Cody rolls his eyes and grins at me, heading off across the grass without waiting to see if Jack can manage to move me.

"Thanks," I say to Jack.

"No problem," he says, grunting a little as he struggles to get both of us moving so that we can get in there and start having that great time I promised everyone.

Although I can't imagine the trip can get any better than it's been so far.

NINETEEN

Cody's waiting at the front door when we finally get caught up, which is a good thing because he has all the tickets. We decided to do the first day without costumes because we figured that would give us more time, which now seems like a good call because it's already almost one and we've missed nearly an hour of the afternoon sessions.

We miss another half hour waiting in line before we finally get in.

And then we all just stop and stare.

I've seen comic festivals on TV and the Internet. Much bigger ones than a small city like Bainesville could ever possibly imagine having. I figured that this one would be a mere microcosm of any of those.

If this is small, I can't imagine how crazy the normal-sized festivals are. This is complete chaos! If I was claustrophobic,

I'd be out of here by now, looking for some air because every tiny piece of space in this room is filled by a body. Everyday people hanging out with superheroes and supervillains who are wandering around with characters from virtually every science-fiction movie or show I've ever heard of, and quite a few I obviously haven't. There are also vampires and hobbits, witches and wizards, and all kinds of weird-looking creatures jumping around trying to scare people. Costumes that range from obvious DIY to some that look like they come straight off a movie set. People talking, yelling, laughing. Occasional screams, which I guess mean some creature managed to be more scary than weird. Loud speakers blare unintelligible things that try to compete with all the talking, yelling, laughing, and screaming.

"Oops, sorry man," Darth Vader growls at me as he tries to pass, catching his black robes on the handle of my chair.

"No problem," I say to his back as it disappears into the mass of bodies.

"Holy shit!" Cody is just standing there, like the townie that he is, eyes bugging and mouth actually hanging open. Jack is standing slightly behind him, trying to see everything at once and bouncing around like a bobblehead of himself.

"Seriously! Do you know where you want to go first?" I poke Cody in the side, trying to get him to focus on me and close his mouth. People are starting to notice us, which is less than cool, since there is a whole hell of a lot to see here that's more interesting than three small-town losers looking like lost puppies at a dog show.

"Ow! That hurt! Stop poking me!" Cody rubs his side as I

grab the map and schedule out of his hand and start trying to figure out what's happening where and when.

"There's a panel discussion starting in about half an hour. Um, there's a video game demo going on somewhere. I'd like to see that. Oh, and a costume competition later that could be cool. I guess you want to do photos tomorrow with your own costume on, right?"

Cody grabs the schedule back and stares at it. Jack is still just standing there staring with big eyes. I reach over and tap him on the hand.

"It's cool, isn't it?"

"It's totally crazy. I don't know what I was expecting, but it wasn't this," he says.

"Me neither. I figured little Bainesville wouldn't attract this many people. I guess the die-hard nerds will go anywhere."

"Nerds nothing. Have you seen some of the girls wandering around?" Cody takes a deep breath and then grins. "This is awesome. Let's go!"

He heads off into the crowd, as I try to navigate behind him without wheeling over any capes or cloaks. Jack walks beside me, neck twisting, as he tries to see in all directions at once.

"Where exactly are we going?" I ask Cody, who just keeps walking without answering. I'm guessing my voice disappeared into the endless mass of torsos that stream by my eye level.

"Ryan asked you where we're going!" Jack says loudly. Cody stares back at him, surprised as if he forgot Jack was with us.

"I think the video game demo is right up there, if we can get close enough to see anything. We can check it out while we wait for the panel discussion."

"Panel discussion?" Jack asks.

"It's when the cast of a movie or TV show sit and talk about their characters or story lines. They usually take questions from the audience, too," I tell him because Cody doesn't.

"Oh." He sounds thrilled.

"It's right up there. Here, Ryan, let me help you," Cody says, grabbing the handles of my chair and starting to push me through. People look down, annoyed, as they feel me brush up against them, but then most of them kind of step aside when they see the wheelchair.

Cody's taking full advantage of my being in a chair. Shocking.

"Handicapped parking." Cody grins widely. Jack looks annoyed. I *feel* annoyed, but it's not worth getting into it with Cody right now.

Besides, he does have a point because now we can all see what's going on.

We sit and watch as some guy in full costume demonstrates the levels and graphics of a game on the giant 3D screen. I bet it wouldn't look nearly as cool on my fifteen-inch desktop screen at home. But the game still looks amazing.

"Okay, enough of that. Let's go."

We aren't even halfway through the demo, and I was just starting to figure it out and get curious about the next level, when Cody turns away, pushing himself through the crowd.

He's apparently forgotten about the benefits of using me as a battering ram, so I'm left to try to navigate my way through on my own if I want to stick with him.

"Here." Jack steps behind me and helps me through, trying to keep up with Cody, who is now hopping through the crowd like he's been doing it his whole life.

"Man, that guy is hyper!" Jack says, weaving me around a couple of old-school Trekkies who have to jump out of the way.

"Yup. He should have worn a Tigger suit."

"I don't see too many Winnie the Pooh characters here. It would have been funny though." Jack laughs.

"What did you decide on for tomorrow?" I ask him, raising my voice so that he can hear.

"Oh, just something boring and lame. Not sure I'll even wear it. I'll show you later at your friend's house."

My friend's house. Right. I haven't told him about the plan change yet.

I don't think now is the time. I'd rather not have to scream it at him.

We keep weaving and wobbling through, trying to keep Cody's back in our sights. He's tall enough, but it's hard to keep track of him with so much to look at between us and him.

"I can't see him, but I can see the sign for the panel thing," Jack says, turning me to the left and just missing a giant 3D cardboard cutout of the next big movie *coming to a theater near you.*

It looks like a cool movie, except that there aren't any theaters near us. The nearest actual movie theater to our town is almost an hour away, so we don't watch a lot of movies until we can download them. We're always behind the rest of the world.

We make it to the panel discussion room, which of course is packed with people in front of us because we stopped to watch the demo instead of coming straight here. Cody is waiting at the door.

"I'll take him," he says to Jack. I shake my head.

"No way. Once is enough for the whole crippled guy to the front routine, Cody. I'm fine back here. You can do what you want."

"Fine. Whatever. I can get to the front on my own." He doesn't invite Jack to come with him. Jack doesn't look like he cares.

Cody takes off, slaloming his way through the bodies like they're moguls on a ski hill. Jack leans back against the wall with his arms folded, and I just sit and listen because all I can see is a bunch of multi-colored butts.

It's a show I watch regularly, and it's interesting for a while to hear the actors talking about their roles and giving hints about what might be coming next in the various story lines.

Jack seems bored. I don't think he watches the show.

The question and answer part starts and I'm pretty sure Cody's voice is the first one I hear. I can't make out the question but everyone laughs. Now I'm sure it was Cody.

The whole thing lasts about twenty minutes. Jack looks like he's actually starting to fall asleep standing up.

"I'm back. That was awesome! There's a food court thing in the main room, and it's right next to all the display tables with shit you can buy. I'm totally starved." Cody is basically vibrating with the need to move on to the next activity.

"I could eat. What about you, Jack?"

He blinks at me a couple of times. Probably waking up.

"Sure, whatever." He shrugs. Cody stands with his back to Jack and makes a face at me.

"All right. I have the map so follow me," he says, taking off again. It would be so much easier to track him if he did come in a Tigger costume. He'd be the only one. It's going to be even harder finding him tomorrow because every second guy here is dressed as Captain America. A few girls, too.

I've noticed several people dressed in a costume opposite to what you would expect them to be in, gender-wise. I wasn't expecting that. I saw a female Harry Potter hanging out with a male Hermione, and even a guy dressed as Wonder Woman.

I wonder if Jack has noticed.

We head into a big open room, which I assume is the skating rink most of the time seeing as there are bleachers all around it for watching games. Even though it's still filled with people, it doesn't feel quite as cramped as the rest of the building, and I actually feel like I can move without running into anyone.

There are tables all around the outside with merchandise on them, and at the far end there's a bunch of food trucks sending out smells that are making my stomach complain loudly about the lack of attention I've been paying to it.

We head straight to the food, ignoring the tables that will later probably completely drain Cody's wallet. Cody gets there first and lines up with the rest of the people looking to eat giant Polish sausages with masses of sauerkraut.

"I don't really like sausages. I'm going to get some Chinese food," Jack says, gesturing toward a truck advertising stir-fry and egg rolls. I go with him. I'd rather have a sausage, but stir-fry is probably safer in this place anyway.

Jack orders for both of us because it's easier that way.

"I'll get this," he says, waving me away when I try to hand him some money.

"Okay, but I'll pay for you later then."

"Deal."

We get our food and look for Cody. It doesn't seem like there's much chance of actually finding a table to eat at. It's not a problem for me, because I'm already sitting down, but Jack looks like he could use a break from standing around.

"Over here!" Cody's voice pierces its way through the eating noises. He's standing on a table, waving his arms at us. Jack just shakes his head.

"Nothing like making sure the whole world notices us."

"Yeah, well, that's just Cody being...Cody, I guess," I say as we make our way across the room. No one actually seems to care. They're all too focused on eating and talking and making sure everyone else notices how cool they look to pay attention to three little dweebs from nowheresville.

"Hey. So, this is Clare a.k.a. Rogue. And this is Sophia a.k.a. Storm. Or the other way around." Cody is sharing a chair with one girl and gesturing toward another sitting beside her at the end of a table with about a dozen people sitting at it. Both girls are in costume and give us big smiles.

"You're right, he is cute. I love red hair on a guy," Sophia or Clare says, smiling directly at me. I just stare at her trying to think of something intelligent to say while my cheeks start heating up. The girl cuddling with Cody looks at my chair, checking out my legs for a few seconds before looking up at Jack.

"You can share Clare's seat," she says to him, gesturing toward the girl who likes red hair. Jack clutches his food against his chest, shaking his head.

"No, I'm fine standing up," he says, heading over to lean against the wall behind the table.

"So, Cody says you're on the swim team together. That's cool." Clare smiles at me again. This time I remember to smile back.

"Yeah. I guess so." *I guess so? I guess I'm on the swim team or I guess it's cool? Smooth, Ryan.*

"Of course it is. Any team that has me as a captain is going to be the best," Cody says, helping himself to some fries off the plate of the girl—Sophia, obviously—who he's practically sitting on top of. Steve would be interested to know that Cody has been self-promoted to team captain. Especially since we've never had a team captain before, seeing as Steve believes there should only be one person in charge, namely the coach.

"Right. *Captain* Cody. Definitely the best." I shake my head at him. For some reason that makes everyone laugh. Including me.

"So, Sophia and I are going to the costume competition after lunch. You guys want to come and watch and then maybe hang out for the afternoon?" Clare smiles at me for the third time. I'm pretty sure I'm blushing, which is never my best look because bright red and bright orange tend to clash. I try to concentrate on eating for a few seconds, chewing slowly so that I can get my face under control.

"Sure," I say too quickly so that I swallow and talk at the same time, making myself choke like an idiot. I lean forward to try to catch some air and hide my red, sweaty face at the same time.

"Are you okay?" Clare says, coming over and patting me on the back. I wave my hand at her as I try to stop myself from hacking up a lung.

"Fine. Just swallowed the wrong way." I wipe at the tears that decided to join the party and make my face look even stupider. My nose is probably running too. *I am such a sexy guy.*

"He just gets all choked up around beautiful women," Cody says helpfully, which makes everyone laugh again. I laugh too, but this time I'm faking it because I don't want the girls to know how stupid I feel. I sit up straight again, wiping at my face and trying to get everything under control.

"So, are we on for the afternoon?" Sophia asks. Cody looks at me with a big shit-eating smile, wiggling his eyebrows and nodding. I clear my throat, hoping I can answer without throwing up or something.

"Sure. Just let me check with Jack." Who I just remembered is behind us by himself trying to eat rice standing up. I look over my shoulder but I can't see him. I turn my chair completely around, scanning the wall as if somehow he slid down to another spot. Still no Jack.

"He isn't here." I turn back to Cody who is busy whispering something into Sophia's left ear. "Cody! Jack isn't here!"

"He's probably just in the can. He'll find us. Go on ahead, ladies. I'll catch up. We don't want to be late." Cody stands up and offers a hand to each of the girls, who both laugh and stand up with a little curtsy thing before heading off toward the exit.

"We have to look for him. He won't know where we are. I think there's something wrong!" I shout at his back. He turns and glares at me.

"Nothing is wrong except that you're acting like your mother, worrying about the guy like he's some baby. I'm going with them. I told you it should have been just us." He turns back with a big smile, picking up the pace until he joins the girls. He hooks an elbow with each of them before heading off into the crowd.

I watch them go and then look around the room full of people, none of whom seem to be Jack. Where the *hell* is he?

TWENTY

He's just not here. He could be anywhere!

It's not like he was having any fun. He's probably upset.

I take out my phone and dial his number. It rings about six times and then goes straight to voicemail. I think about texting, but if he's not answering when I call he'll likely ignore a text, too. *If* he's ignoring me.

Maybe he *can't* answer.

Shit.

Cody was right. This was such a stupid idea. What was I thinking taking some messed up, suicidal kid on a trip out of town?

I wheel around the massive room, searching every face that isn't covered by makeup or a mask. The panic is taking hold, making it feel like I'm back in the river trying to find a yellow skirt floating underwater.

It was so obvious he wasn't enjoying himself. Any idiot could see that. But I just ignored him because there were a couple of pretty girls at the table.

How long was it? A few minutes, tops. Right?

Did he tell me where he was going and I just didn't hear him?

Was he upset?

What am I supposed to do now? I doubt they have one of those lost and found desks like at shopping malls where you can put on an announcement for your lost kid.

Then again, maybe they do. After all there are a lot of people here.

I could have him paged.

Then I'd find out Cody is right and he was just in the bathroom, and he'll be embarrassed that I paged him and I'll make everything worse than it already is.

I won't have him paged.

I'll just look for him. *Calm down and just look!*

It's not like there's a large body of water around here for him to wander into. At least I don't think there is.

Just a giant highway five minutes down the road.

Is there a river in Bainesville? Why don't I know? Why didn't I find that out?

What if he's so upset he decided to find some way to finish what he started?

Why the hell did his mother and counselor let him come with us in the first place? Seriously irresponsible.

My head spins around every nightmare scenario as I spin

down every open space I can find. The food smells are starting to make my stomach churn. First I choke and now I feel like I'm going to puke. This is ridiculous.

He isn't in this room. I've been around it, like, ten times. If he was in the bathroom, he'd have been back near the table long ago. He obviously left.

Maybe he just wanted to look around on his own.

Sure he did. Because he's so fascinated by fucking Comic Con that he decided to brave wandering around in the middle of a gazillion strangers.

I manage to find my way out of the ice-rink-turned-cafeteria and head down into the maze of side rooms that have the other events going on. I look in one doorway and see people standing on a stage in full costume while the audience cheers and claps. Cody is obviously in there. I should go in and kick his ass. Or punch him in the gut anyway. He's such a prick. He should be helping me look for Jack.

Except that he didn't want Jack with us in the first place, and it would only piss him off more than he already is if he spends his whole first day running around in circles.

I didn't think about this when I came up with my brilliant plan.

That's not true. I did think about it but I decided I was being paranoid. He told me the water was like a spur of the moment thing. He didn't plan it. He wasn't trying to kill himself. Not really.

That's what he said. I think.

I don't know anymore!

What if he planned this whole thing? What if that's why he worked on his counselor and his mother to let him go to something he obviously has no interest in? So that he could actually…what did he say?

Make the hurting stop.

Which means making his own hurting stop because he'll be making a whole world of hurt for everyone else if he actually goes off somewhere and figures out a way to end it.

And it'll be my fault.

Where could he have gone?

Obviously not inside the building. I have to go look outside.

Maybe he's just getting some air.

Maybe he's jumping off the roof.

Shut up, Ryan!

I consider trying to find Cody because he's a hell of a lot faster running around outside than I can be wheeling over the rough pavement and grass. But even if he would consider helping me just to be a decent human, I don't think I can find my way back to him at this point.

I can vaguely see a red EXIT sign in the distance and I head toward it, hoping it's a way outside. It takes a few minutes, but I manage to get there and am totally relieved to find that it's the door we came in.

I have to show the ink stamp on my hand to leave. The guy tells me that I have to get back in less than an hour or today's stamp will expire and I won't be able to come back in to have more fun.

Outside, I sit for a moment, trying to slow my insides down so I can think. Jack is a little guy and not exactly an athlete. He can't be too far away, right?

This is stupid. I'm sitting staring at a giant parking lot full of cars and trucks. There are roads on all sides of the building. There's a great big field on the other side of one of the roads that leads to more roads. Even if I had a car and could drive it, I wouldn't have any idea where to start looking.

I can't calm down. My heart is pounding like I just finished the 800 and my stomach is jumping around so much it feels like it's trying to exit my body. *What the hell am I supposed to do now?*

I close my eyes, willing my body to just slow the hell down so I can think. Deep breaths. Slow breaths.

"Ryan? What are you doing out here?"

The voice makes me jump as my eyes fly open, everything revving up to full speed again.

"Jack! Where have you been?" The words fly at him, double-edged and sharp so that he actually takes a step back to avoid getting stabbed.

"I told you I was going for a walk. I got talking to someone and it took a little longer than I expected." He looks offended. I try to get my voice under control so he doesn't know how upset I am.

"I didn't hear you say anything."

"I haven't been gone that long. I'm sorry you didn't hear me. It was noisy in there and you were…busy."

He waits for me to say something. Anything I want to say is some version of *I was scared you had gone off to kill yourself.*

156

Since I don't think any version of that is going to make this day get better, I keep my mouth shut for a couple of seconds.

"What, are you pissed at me or something?"

I am pissed at him. Completely and totally. Pissed at him. Pissed at Cody. And pissed at myself.

"No, no it's fine. You just surprised me. I thought you might have got lost with so many people here or something." Pieces of the truth.

"Well, I kind of did. But it's okay because I actually met someone interesting. We got talking. I guess I was gone longer than I thought." He's trying to look apologetic…I think…but it also seems like he's in a better mood than he's been in the whole trip so far.

"Oh?" I say, thinking about Clare and how I missed the chance to talk to her. Not that I would have managed to come up with anything very interesting. Although she seemed to enjoy my choking routine.

"Yeah. I was walking around outside, trying to get back to the right entrance when this guy came up to me and asked if I was lost, and I said I was, and then we just started talking." He stops and looks at me, as if he isn't sure he should keep going.

"And?"

"Well, he was wearing a costume. A Wonder Woman costume." He stops again.

"Oh, yeah. I think I saw him earlier. Nice legs. For a guy, I mean!" I add the last part so quickly that Jack laughs at me.

"Yeah, right. I don't even think he was the only Wonder Woman guy here today. I didn't expect any guys would be dressed in women's costumes, but no one seems to care who's wearing what here."

"I noticed that too. I bet Wonder *Man* wouldn't go over very well back at school though." He snorts, making me laugh.

"No, definitely not! Anyway, I asked him about his costume and if it means anything. He just kind of laughed at me and said that it means he likes to wear whatever he wants to wear. He told me some guys who cross-dress at these festivals are gay, but not all of them. *He's* gay though."

"That's cool." *Is that the right thing to say?*

"Yeah, it is to me. I've never actually talked to anyone else who's gay in my life. At least, not that I know of. And I told him that I'm gay too, because…well, just because it felt okay to do it. Safe, I guess. Does that make sense?"

"Yeah, of course." Jack smiles a bit like he's pleased with my answer.

"Anyway, he, Caleb, goes to the college here and he was telling me that there's actually a group on campus that gives support and advice to people. They put on social stuff, too, that anyone from the city can come to. They even have a float in the Pride Parade every year." Jack sounds amazed by everything he's telling me, as if he's describing some kind of magical world that he'd never imagined could actually exist.

"He said that there's a pretty high level of acceptance in this city, but that there are still homophobic assholes around. But the support networks make it easier." He pauses for a second and looks at me. "I'm thinking that I should apply to go to college here."

"Sounds like a pretty good idea," I say. "I've been thinking about it too."

"That would be cool. I'm not sure my mom even wants me to go to college though. But even if I didn't move here for school, maybe I could find a job or something." He sounds almost hopeful.

"Once you're old enough you can do what you want." *I'm planning on it.*

"Yeah, well, the trick will be surviving Thompson Mills until I'm old enough to leave." He looks down at the ground, kicking at some gravel and making a small cloud of dust.

I open my mouth to say something encouraging but get instantly drowned out.

"What are you guys doing outside? I've been looking for you two idiots for ages. If you hadn't noticed, the festival…and the girls…are all inside the building." Cody comes toward us. He has a big, goofy hat on that I don't recognize from anything I've ever read or seen. He's strutting toward us like he's the best-dressed guy in the place—big grin on his face and stupid hat wobbling every time he takes a step.

Jack takes one look and actually bursts out laughing. I join in and Cody just glares at both of us in complete disgust, shaking his head, which makes the stupid hat bounce around even more, so that we laugh even harder as we follow him back into the fantasy factory.

TWENTY-ONE

"Okay, let's see if we can find the car and then head to Shady Rest," Cody says as we're basically swept out of the building by the crowd at the end of the day. We managed to salvage the rest of the evening by getting a few autographs, meeting up with Sophia and Clare again for a while, and then watching the final costume competition of the day. Cody didn't give Jack any grief for disappearing, and Jack stopped looking like he wanted the floor to open up and swallow him. So, a pretty good end to an otherwise bizarre and stress-filled first day.

Until now.

I forgot to tell Jack about the motel. Again. He's going to be royally pissed with me. I don't think he'll believe some big lie about plans changing at the last minute.

"Shady what?" Jack asks. "Your friend lives somewhere shady?"

"About that…" I start.

"We aren't going to Jacob's house with his mommy and daddy because we aren't twelve, and this is a road trip. I booked us a motel," Cody finishes. Jack looks at Cody and just nods.

"Okay. My mom just texted me and I told her we're fine and heading out for the night. She'll never know the difference. That's good enough."

I look from him to Cody in surprise. Cody grins and starts to whistle as he makes his way over to our car. Jack has the job of helping me across the grass again, and I keep waiting for him to say something, but there's nothing. He has no problem with it. I was so sure he'd be upset that I've been hiding it for weeks and worrying about it most of the day. And all he says is "*okay*"?

Cody's right. I am acting like my mother. This seriously needs to stop.

We have to move to the side and wait for a while so that Cody can back the car up long enough for me to get loaded back in. The place is pretty much deserted by the time we're able to do that, and it's getting really dark.

"We need to stop for some food on the way. I already have some drinks but we might want more than just the beer. I'm not sure how good the water is going to be in this place," Cody says.

"Sounds like a nice place," Jack says from the back seat. Cody laughs.

"Yup. It's the fanciest motel in town—so the website says."

We drive ten minutes to the outskirts of the city, stopping along the way so that Cody can run in and grab food and pop at a small grocery store. He settles back down in the car, tossing a bag into the back seat, filled with what looks like enough junk food to make my mother write an entire lecture series on the evils of eating garbage.

"There it is," he says as a low building comes into sight with a big neon sign that says SHA RES OTEL.

"I think there are some letters missing," Jack says, stating the obvious.

"Looks *fancy* to me," I tell Cody. I can see a pool at the front, with a few sad-looking lawn chairs sprinkled around it, but it doesn't seem to have any water in it.

That might be a good thing.

"I'll run in and get our key. I got two double beds and a cot thing. Should be cool." Cody parks in front of the door marked FRONT OFFICE and bounces in. He's back in a couple of minutes, gets back into the car, and drives down to park in front of number 19.

He brings me my chair and helps me transfer, and then we grab our bags. He unlocks the door, and we head in.

I can just make out two beds and a cot that pretty much fill the entire room. There's a small TV on a dresser in front of one of the beds. It's hotter than our classrooms on the hottest day of the year and smells just as bad.

"Ta-dah!" Cody flings his bags onto the nearest bed as he turns on the lights. In the glare of the bare bulbs, it looks pretty much the way it smells.

"Nice," I say, trying to sound positive. I definitely think we'll avoid drinking the water.

"Yeah, really nice," Jack says. "I'll take the cot." He

obviously got a good look at those beds. I'm not sure who slept there last, but whoever it was left an impression.

I put my bag down on the floor and head for the bathroom.

"Um, Cody?"

"Yeah?"

"Did you mention to the front desk that I'm in a chair?"

He looks over from where he's fiddling with the TV. "No. I forgot all about it. Was I supposed to tell them?"

"Well, it might have been a good idea. I can't get into the bathroom. I'd really rather not have to be lifted in and out. You'd probably drop me on the floor."

"Oh. Shit. Well, then. I guess I'd better talk to them, see if there's another room with a wider door. Be right back." He smiles cheerfully, as if it's no big deal that I literally can't go to the bathroom by myself, and heads out the door.

Jack sits on the one wooden chair, shaking his head.

"So, this is better than your friend's place how?" he asks.

"It's all about independence and drinking beer, I think. Although, at this moment, I'm not so sure *independence* is the right word, seeing as I'm going to need help getting into the bathroom if we can't find another room."

"So…Cody is your *best* friend?"

"Yup. Since grade school."

"But he forgot about your chair?"

"Yeah. Not exactly forgot. He knows it's there, but a lot of the time he just doesn't think about it. Could be why he's my best friend."

Jack looks like he wants to ask another question, but

instead, he takes over trying to get some reception on the TV. Cody comes back a couple of minutes later, grinning from ear to ear.

"So, because they *forgot* that I told them you're handicapped and everything, they decided to upgrade us to the Superior Room, which is fully accessible…and they're not charging us anything extra for it. Room 26." He grabs his bag, spins around, and heads back out the door. Jack and I grab our stuff and follow him.

"You guys walk down. Here's the key. I'll bring the car."

"I doubt the Superior Room is much better than this one," he says, as he starts walking down the pathway.

"No, but if it means I can piss on my own, it's all good."

"Yeah, I can understand that."

It takes about twenty seconds to find the Superior Room. Cody is already there, of course. He comes to the door and invites us in like some kind of doorman at a fancy hotel.

"Here you'll find the couch. Yes, boys, we have a couch. A fold-out couch, no less. With a little table in front of it. And over here there's a TV that's actually working and big enough to watch a movie on. And down here is a fridge, which is good because the beer has been in my car all day and is a little warmer than I like it. Oh, and best of all…Ryan, come with me."

He walks over to the end of the room, where a nice wide door leads into a bathroom that is actually big enough for me to turn around in. It even has a grab bar on the wall.

"This is definitely superior."

"Right? This is perfect. I'm so glad you're in a wheelchair!"

He turns away and runs over to the beds, flinging himself down on one. Jack looks like he's wondering why I don't throw something in Cody's face.

"He doesn't mean it like that," I start to explain, but Cody interrupts.

"I hate when you talk about me behind my back...especially when I'm lying right here. *What* didn't I mean?"

"You didn't mean you're actually glad I can't walk." He sits up and looks at me, kind of staring at my legs like he just noticed them and figured out why I sit in this chair.

"Of course not. I know it sucks to be you. But it comes in handy sometimes."

"Cody!" Jack says, sounding shocked.

"*Cody* what? What's your problem? Ryan doesn't mind it. If he's cool with being in the chair, why're you all bent out of shape about it?"

"Well, I'm not always exactly *cool* with being in the chair," I tell him. He looks confused.

"What do you mean?"

"I mean, sometimes I really wish like hell I could just jump out of this damn thing and run down the street. I wish I didn't wear braces and that my legs and feet weren't all spazzed out all the time so that they hurt and make it impossible for me to stand on them." The words spill out of my mouth, surprising all three of us.

"Hey, man. Sorry. I wasn't trying to upset you. I didn't know you felt like that. I mean, I figured you've always been in the chair so you're used to it or whatever."

"I am used to it. I don't cry every morning because I have to go in it. This is my life and I totally accept that. But it doesn't mean I don't feel like I'm missing out on something at the same time."

Jack's big eyes stare as if he's trying to memorize everything I say. Cody, on the other hand, is looking at the ceiling with his eyes half shut. I don't even know if he heard me or not.

I know Cody wasn't trying to piss me off. He's the one person outside of my family who I can always trust to treat me like everybody else. I'm not sure why I thought he needed a lecture from me. Maybe meeting Clare today has made me hypersensitive or something.

We're quiet for a minute, then Cody rolls off the bed and stands up. "I put three of the beers in the little freezer deal at the top of the fridge. Should be cold enough to drink by now. I think it's time to have one and find something brainless to watch on TV." He heads to the fridge, stopping for just a second to punch me lightly on the arm when we make eye contact.

"Okay, one for you!" He throws a lukewarm can into my lap.

"One for you." He hands the second one to Jack. "And one for me. Now I'll put the other three in here. Sucks that I could only grab six. My brother is freakishly obsessed with keeping track of his booze. I had to sneak these out one at a time when his drinking friends were over so he wouldn't notice."

"I'm good with just one. Actually, I'm fine with pop," Jack says, looking at the warm can in his hand.

"No. It's fine. Come on, drink up." Cody opens his can and tips it back, draining half of it with one go. I open mine and take a swig. I like a cold beer once in a while, when my mother is nowhere close by, but this is not cold beer. This is warm beer. It tastes gross, but I'm going to drink it anyway because it seems to mean a lot to Cody. I grab a handful of chips out of the bag Jack opened, shove them in my mouth, and wash them down with the beer. The combination isn't bad.

I wave to Jack and show him my trick, pointing at the chip bag and then the beer can. He nods and grins, grabbing some chips and then drinking some beer. He does it too fast and starts choking.

"What are you doing?" Cody asks him, turning away from the TV long enough to notice the coughing and the spewing of chips.

"He seems to be choking," I tell him. "You could do something."

"He's just coughing. It's different. You remember lifesaving classes? Oh, right, of course you do." He shakes his head and walks over to Jack, smacking him on the back a few times, increasing the force of each hit until Jack pushes his hand away in self defense.

"I'm fine," he gasps. "Just swallowed the wrong way."

"Good because it would suck if you died right here. Then we'd get in all kinds of shit because we're supposed to be at some guy's house, right?"

Jack looks at him, tears streaming down his face as he tries to get his throat working again.

"Cody, you are such an ass!" I can't believe he would say something like that to Jack.

"What are you talking about? I said it's good he *didn't* die. Seriously Ryan, you need to calm down. First you have a total freak fit because the guy went for a walk and now you're upset because I said the word *died* in front of him. If you're so worried, why'd you bring him in the first place?"

TWENTY-TWO

The room goes silent except for the background noise coming from the TV. Cody is glaring at me. I'm glaring at him. Jack is glaring at me.

Two against one.

"I thought you said it was fine. That you weren't worried when you couldn't find me. That's what you said." Jack's eyes are getting into black hole territory.

Shit and double shit.

"I'm sorry. I didn't want you to know I was acting stupid. You didn't answer your phone when I called, and I just thought maybe you were upset because we were ignoring you, and I guess I was a bit…panicky looking for you. I did not freak!" I'm still glaring at Cody even though I'm talking to Jack.

"Yeah, you did." Cody is obviously tired of the glaring game and is back to concentrating on TV.

"I didn't answer my phone because I was talking to someone and didn't think it was a big deal, seeing as the person calling *wasn't* my mom."

"Nope, it was just someone acting like your mom," Cody says helpfully as he shoves a handful of chips in his mouth. If I could reach something worth throwing at him, I would.

"Well I already have a mom who worries about me all the time and doesn't understand anything about me. I don't need you doing that shit too. I thought you were my friend. Or at least someone who treats me like a normal person."

Jack shakes his head and takes a swig of his beer, making a face as it goes down. "Tastes like warm piss," he says.

Cody laughs, spraying chips all over the bed. "When did you ever drink warm piss?"

"Very funny." Jack grabs his own handful and starts chewing, still glaring at me with seriously angry eyes. I clear my throat, hoping to loosen up a few words that won't make him angrier.

"I'm sorry. I shouldn't have acted like that. I guess since I invited you, I felt…responsible or something."

Jack swallows and wipes his hand across his mouth.

"I'm responsible for myself. You don't need to take care of me."

"Except when you're drowning in the river," Cody says, never taking his eyes off the TV. "Then he kinda needs to take care of you. You seriously can't swim?"

"Not really. I've always hated it so I never really tried to learn." Jack answers the question while ignoring the first part of what Cody said.

"I can't imagine hating the water! I've always loved it. If you hate it, why the hell would you pick drowning as the way to go?"

"*Cody!*" I yell, but he ignores me.

"I didn't *pick* it. It just kind of happened." Jack's voice is softer and lower, dipping down into the danger zone.

"You just *kind of* walked into the river and almost drowned until the hero of the century rolled in on top of you. That sounds a bit like bullshit to me. Sounds like you were trying to off yourself, like everyone says. Is it because you're gay?" Cody is still looking at the TV, as if the things he's saying are casual comments that don't need his full attention.

Jack looks over at me, long enough to make the hairs on the back of my neck stand up. I'm wondering if he wants me to say something to shut Cody up or if he just wants everyone to shut themselves up. After what seems like forever, he finally takes a deep breath and turns his eyes back to Cody.

"Not because I'm gay. Because I'm gay in a town where no one wants anyone to be anything different from everyone else, and I can't even tell my own mother who I am because she would never understand and would probably kick me out!"

Cody finally turns away from the TV and looks directly at Jack. I just sit there with my mouth hanging open at the shock of hearing Jack admit he's gay to Cody. I can't believe he did that.

"Your mother wouldn't kick you out. I do all kinds of crap my mother hates, but she would never kick me out. Not for more than an hour or two anyway."

"This is different. This is not me *doing* something she doesn't like. This is my whole life. Myself. Who I am. Which most people in our town think is something dirty or gross. Including you, by the way."

Cody sits with his mouth shut for a while before answering.

"I don't know if being gay is gross or dirty. Most guys I know *do* think it would be gross to have some other guy hit on them. I guess that includes me because I told Ryan I was worried you would hit on me." Cody looks pretty uncomfortable.

"Don't worry. You're not my type."

Cody seems surprised and a little offended. I accidentally start laughing but try to cover it up with a cough.

"So, you like guys and I like girls. I guess it isn't really that big a deal." Cody doesn't look convinced by his own words, but I'm guessing his brain is going to end up burying itself if he has to think any more deeply about this.

"Except no one tries to beat the shit out of you for liking girls." Jack's voice is bitter.

"Well, that depends on what girl I'm liking. Sometimes boyfriends, dads, or brothers aren't too happy with me."

"Cody. It's not the same," I finally interrupt the conversation that I never expected these two guys to have.

"Now, here's a whole different example," Cody says, neatly changing direction as he gestures toward me with both hands. "This here is a guy who likes girls but never actually talks to any. So he is one of the last virgins at our high school because he's the world's biggest chickenshit when it comes to the female of the species."

"Shut up, Cody!" I grab a pillow and throw it at his face. "You don't understand anything. You have no idea what it's like trying to find a girl to like me when I'm sitting in this chair."

Cody has no idea why I'm a virgin. I mean, aside from the fact that I've never had an actual girlfriend. The truth is I am scared shitless of getting intimate with someone. What would happen if I finally found someone who wanted to sleep with me and my legs decided to spaz out at some significant moment? And I'm scared that if I'm worrying about spazzing out, I won't be able to do anything else right, and she'll be upset with me... or worse, laugh at me. What if I'm just a big joke in bed?

Besides, I seem to have enough trouble finding someone to date, let alone sleep with. I'm fairly certain that Clare is the first girl I've ever met who didn't look at my chair first and my face second. It's always been pretty obvious that most girls are uncomfortable with the idea of dating a guy in a chair.

Cody interrupts my self-pity fest with a disgusted snort.

"You use that chair like a crutch."

"What? That doesn't even make sense!"

"I mean, you use it as an excuse. Lots of guys are scared of screwing up when they meet a pretty face. Not me, of course, but lots of other guys have to figure out how to get girls to like them. You just need some confidence in yourself. Eventually you'll find someone who doesn't mind the chair or your ugly orange hair." He messes up my hair and I smack his hand away. Hard.

"Thanks. You're always *so* supportive."

"Yeah, you're lucky to have me!" Cody goes over to the

fridge. "Who's ready for more beer?" He looks at us both.

"I'm good," says Jack. I shake my head. Cody reaches in and grabs himself a beer and then stands there looking at me for a second.

"Ryan, Clare thought you were super cute. Her words not mine. Sophia thinks I'm totally awesome. My words not hers, but I could tell she was thinking it. They want to spend the day with us tomorrow, so maybe you could practice not feeling sorry for yourself and actually enjoy being somewhere away from Thompson Mills with a couple of girls who might be willing to put up with you."

I take this in for a few seconds. Cody might be doing his best to piss me off but he's making sense at the same time. Besides, I can never stay mad at him for more than five minutes. He won't let me.

"I guess," I say, "but it doesn't sound like much fun for Jack."

"Well, I was trying to find a way to talk to you about that. Caleb invited me to spend the day with him and some of his friends. I wasn't really sure at first about spending the whole day with them, but I've thought about it and I think I'd like to give it a try. Maybe we could just keep in touch by text and meet up later in the day—if that's okay?" Jack looks a little embarrassed to be asking.

"Oh, okay. That's cool." I don't really know if it's cool or not. I want to ask him if he's sure it's a safe idea. But if I say anything about it, I'll be accused of morphing into my mother again.

"I guess we'll hang out with Clare and Sophia then," I say instead, looking over at Cody.

"Good plan. In the meantime, could we stop with the heavy crap and just have a couple of drinks and watch the rest of this movie? We're acting like a room full of girls," Cody says.

"I thought you liked girls."

"I like being *with* girls, not turning into one," says the master of sensitivity. "Oh, by the way, what about you, Jack? Have you managed to stop being a virgin yet?"

"Cody!" My voice squeaks like it's decided to go through puberty again. The guy has no boundaries at all!

"It's okay. He'll just find another way to ask and probably in a more embarrassing situation, so I might as well answer now. No, Cody, I haven't stopped being a virgin yet. Seeing as I'm pretty sure I'm the only gay guy in town, it's a little tough to find someone to stop being a virgin with." Cody looks at him, nodding seriously.

"Anyway, Cody, can we just stop with the heavy crap and watch TV?" Jack says, smiling but looking like he wants to punch him at the same time.

I know exactly how he feels.

TWENTY-THREE

By about two a.m. we finally decide to try sleeping. We had ordered a pizza after the first movie and by the end of the second one had managed to eat everything we'd bought or brought. The second beer was cold enough that it tasted half decent, which was too bad because Cody grabbed mine about halfway through and drained it, since he had finished his hours earlier.

We open up the hideaway bed in the couch, which Jack volunteers to use, leaving Cody and me with the two double beds. The room goes silent within seconds and I figure both Cody and Jack have passed out. The beer must have had a relaxing effect on my legs because even they fall asleep right away. I should mention it to my doctor as a therapy option.

The alarm I set on my phone wakes us up six hours later. The morning session is scheduled for ten, which should give us time to get in costume and eat some breakfast.

"So, who wants the bathroom first?" Cody asks, jumping out of bed with an annoying level of energy. I'm tired and now my legs are cramping, probably because the bed seems to be made of rocks. I guess it's too early for beer therapy, not that there's any left.

"I'm going to take a few minutes to get up so you go ahead. Unless you want it, Jack?"

"No. I'm good. My mom's already texting me, so I'd better take a minute and answer her." He concentrates on texting for the next few minutes while I concentrate on relaxing my legs and wondering whether my costume is good enough or whether I should just go as me again.

About five minutes pass in silence and then Cody leaps out of the bathroom.

"Captain America at your service!" He bows, sweeping his arm down to the floor. He's got the whole deal on, complete with shield and a few fake muscles thrown in, not that you'd ever get him to admit that.

He actually looks pretty good, not that you'd ever get *me* to admit that. He's already full enough of himself as it is. Cram any more self-confidence in there and he'll explode.

"You're still in bed! Get your ass moving. They have breakfast at this place in a little room behind the office. We have to get there or it'll be gone."

I'm still trying to get my legs calmed down, but there's not much point explaining that to Captain America, who is busy admiring his muscles in the mirror.

"Give me a minute. Why don't you go grab us some stuff and bring it back?"

"Sure. Do you care what you eat?" he asks, standing sideways to check out his profile.

"No, whatever they have is fine. What about you, Jack?" He looks up from his phone.

"Sure, whatever. I'm not that hungry anyway," he says.

"I'll be back!" Cody does a really bad imitation of the Terminator as he heads out of the room, still carrying his shield just in case he has to defend justice on the way to breakfast.

I finally manage to make my body work enough to get out of bed and into my chair.

"I'm going to steal the bathroom for a bit, if that's okay. Try to get my costume on." Jack puts his phone into his pocket and nods.

"No problem."

"Do you have your costume ready? What did you decide on anyway?"

"I had no idea what to wear. I'm not a big fan like you guys. I've seen some of the movies but nothing I've seen before seemed like something I'd be able to pull off. So I just went for the super traditional and bought a cheap Superman costume. Blue spandex and a red cape. Reminded me of Jay the Great."

"Superman is fine. I actually didn't see all that many wandering around yesterday. Maybe going traditional makes you more of an original."

"I guess. But I was thinking I might not wear a costume

at all, if that's okay with you. I'm meeting new people today. I think I just want to go as me."

"Whatever you're comfortable with is cool. I'm starting to think I'd rather just go as me also. I'm having second thoughts about Wolverine in a wheelchair."

"No, you should do it! Cody will kill you if you bail and besides, Wolverine in a wheelchair is awesome. I saw a Batman in a chair, which I thought was incredibly cool."

"Seriously? I wish I had seen that. Sounds almost as cool as a Wonder Woman costume on a guy. If you had known that guys dress up as women characters, would you have tried one?" Jack thinks for a few seconds then shakes his head.

"I wouldn't have had the guts to do that this year. Especially with Cody here. Maybe next year I'll buy a blond wig and a red skirt and use my costume after all." His cheeks pink up a bit, but I just grin at him.

"I'd love to see Cody's reaction to that!"

"Yeah, well, it's enough that he knows I'm gay. Pretty sure he hasn't quite absorbed that one yet. I think we'll keep the rest of it to ourselves for now. Don't want his head to explode."

I laugh as I grab my bag and head for the bathroom to try to transform into someone tough and cool so that Clare won't remember that it's me.

Come to think of it, she's dressed as Rogue, who follows Wolverine around a lot in the movies. This could be perfect. Although from what I saw yesterday, Clare is more of a leader than a follower.

That's cool. I'd be happy following her around.

I pull out the black stretchy costume that's supposed to look like the X-Men in full attack mode. But the pants catch on my braces when I try to pull them up, and I'm left with a bulky-looking mess at the bottom instead of smooth and muscular calves. Not a good start.

The top part goes on fine. There aren't any fake muscles in this one, but it's got enough layers that I look okay from the waist up. Except for the bright red hair and freckles.

I pull out the brown wig and shove it on my head. Great. Now I'm a brown-haired, orange-freckled Wolverine. I take the sideburns out of the bag and put the special glue on so I can attach them to my cheeks. That's a little better but still mostly looks stupid.

I open the door of the bathroom.

"Cody?" I yell out.

"He's not back yet. Must be fighting crime or something," Jack calls back. "Are you okay? Do you need something?"

"I don't know."

"What do you mean? Oh, that's cool." He's at the door of the bathroom, trying to be polite as he looks at my so-called transformation.

"Yeah, the orange freckles and eyebrows really finish it off."

Jack looks at me for a few seconds.

"I can fix that for you," he says, looking a little embarrassed.

"How? Do you have a full-face mask in your bag?"

"No. But I have some makeup. I bought it a while ago." He shrugs, cheeks pink again. "I think I have something that'll cover the freckles. And I can darken the eyebrows, if you want me to try."

I hesitate for a moment, imagining what Cody would do if he came back while Jack was putting makeup on my face.

"I'm pretty sure Hugh Jackman wore makeup in those movies," Jack says, as if he's reading my thoughts and giving me a comeback for Cody.

"Good point. All right. Go for it. It's better than looking like this."

He runs back into the main room, then comes back and dumps a bunch of little bottles and tubes out of a small bag onto the back of the toilet.

"I hide this stuff in my bedroom closet. Which makes sense, I guess, since the rest of me is still basically in there too." He takes a little bottle and shakes it. He pours some beige stuff into his hand.

"Best if you just close your eyes until I'm done. Your mouth, too. I've never practiced on someone else. I don't want to get it anywhere it shouldn't be."

I close everything up and just try to sit still while he does his thing. It feels really strange, and I just focus on hoping Cody stays amused somewhere else for a few more minutes.

"There. It's not perfect but it'll do. You can open your eyes." I open them and look at myself in the bathroom mirror. Jack is standing behind, also looking at me, his eyes a bit worried.

My freckles are completely gone. My cheeks and forehead are one color for the first time in my life, except where he's drawn over my eyebrows and made them dark brown with kind of a slant to make them look more Wolverine-ish. I'm not sure but I think my eyelashes are brown, too, instead of their usual pale orange. The sideburns look better, and I lean forward to see why. It looks like he's sort of sketched in around them, so it seems like they're part of my face, and then drawn in what looks like what my dad calls a five o'clock stubble, which looks real if you don't get too close.

"Wow. That's…amazing! You could do this professionally."

"Makeup artist? Sure. Tell that one to my dad."

"Hey! Where are you guys? I have breakfast!" Cody's voice comes into the room before he does. We both jump, looking guilty, and Jack backs out into the main room quickly as I shut the bathroom door for a second, opening it again as if I was just coming out of the bathroom on my own.

Cody is setting a pile of food down on the TV stand. It looks like bagels and muffins and maybe some cold toast.

"That took a while," I say as I wheel self-consciously across the room. Cody looks at me, eyes tracking up and down, before settling on my face.

"Hey, that doesn't look nearly as lame as I expected."

"Gee, thanks."

"You're welcome. Here's the food. It took a while because there were three very nice ladies there who were in need of some company." He grins.

"Lucky for them Captain America was on the case."

"Totally. Hey, where's your costume?" Cody asks Jack, who's checking out the breakfast options.

"I decided not to bother."

Cody looks at him for a second and then grabs a couple of bagels, holding them on either side of his head. "You could always go as a Princess Leia," he says, laughing at his own joke.

Jack and I don't join in.

"Maybe next year," Jack says in a voice that manages to be sarcastic and serious at the same time.

"Whatever." Cody rolls his eyes as he grabs a muffin and shoves it into his mouth. "Come on, eat something. I *did* go to all the effort of bringing it here," he says, giving us a nice view of muffin mush.

"I think I'll pass on the bagels," Jack says.

"Agreed. Who knows where those hands have been."

Cody picks the two bagels back up and throws them, hitting both of us square in the face. Jack throws his right back, but Cody neatly deflects it with his plastic shield. I just let mine bounce off me and fall to the floor as I take a quick glance in the mirror.

I really hope he didn't ruin my makeup.

TWENTY-FOUR

We find the girls first and then say good-bye to Jack. He looks so nervous about meeting up with that Caleb guy that I want to offer to go with him, but I manage to keep my mouth shut so that Cody won't call me a worried mother in front of Clare.

The first part of the morning seems to disappear in about three seconds. We managed to get a few photos done and are now waiting in a crazy line that looked impossibly long at first but has ended up being pretty close to perfection because it's giving me time to get my brain functioning enough to have a full conversation with Clare. She is the smartest person I think I've ever met, but she seems to find me worth talking to anyway. She's one of those people who knows something about everything but doesn't lord it over you. Little bits of information just seem to pop out of her mouth naturally, as if she had the world's largest storage locker of random facts in her head.

She asks me about my legs so casually, like it's the sort of thing she discusses every day. I tell her I have CP, and she nods and tells me what she knows about it, which is more than anyone else I've ever met outside of the rehab center or doctor's office. She asks me a few questions about things like accessibility where I live and about being on the swim team. I usually hate it when a girl wants to talk about my legs or my wheelchair, or even my swimming. Most of the time, it's an awkward conversation with lots of oh-poor-you or isn't-that-amazing type comments. But Clare isn't acting sympathetic or amazed. She's just…interested.

"You want to hear something cool about Ryan? Tell her about Jack!" Cody interrupts us. He's been running up and down the line, finding other Captain Americas and comparing costumes. Mostly people seem to be laughing at him but a few looked less than thrilled with some of his comments. I keep expecting him to go flying into the air on the end of someone's fist, but so far he seems relatively unscathed by his adventures in bothering people.

"Jack?"

"Yeah. Sir Ryan here saved the guy's life," Cody answers, going down on one knee in front of me with his stupid plastic shield plastered against his chest before I can tell him to shut up.

"Do you mean the guy who was with you yesterday?" Sophia asks, smiling like she does every time he comes anywhere near her. She obviously thinks Cody's the funniest person she's ever met.

Both girls look at me with interest.

I guess it is kind of impressive to rescue someone, whether you're in a chair or not—despite what my little brother thinks. It would be pretty sweet to see the admiration that I figure would come into Clare's eyes if she heard that I actually went into the water to save someone's life.

But Jack's here somewhere, trying to get away from home and everything that went on there. I have no right to bring up something that's more his business than mine.

"No, not him." I decide on a lie. I glare at Cody for a second. I can't see his eyes very well because of his silly mask, but I'm hoping he can read mine. "It was a different guy. There are a few Jacks in our school."

Cody makes a *you're-full-of-shit* face at me. I ignore him, and neither girl notices his expression because they're both focused on me. This is new. Two gorgeous females staring at me while Cody stands around, looking for someone to impress.

"So, tell us about it!" Sophia says as we inch forward in the line. At this rate, we might be here all day.

I can think of worse ways to spend my time.

"It was nothing," I say modestly.

"Says the great hero of Thompson Mills!" I send a *shut-your-mouth* glare at Cody, but he isn't looking my way. He's scoping out another Captain and preparing for battle.

"Thompson Mills. I've heard of that place." Clare stares at me for a second. I can feel myself blushing under the makeup and hope it's thick enough to conceal my impression of a fire truck.

"Oh, I know! I read about it. That was you?" I nod, still being modest and humble about the whole thing.

"What are you talking about?" Sophia asks Clare.

"He's that guy I told you about! Remember? The guy who got himself out of his wheelchair and down into the river from a bridge to save someone. You were a headline in our local paper! It was a pretty ironic one when you think about it." Clare laughs.

"Ironic?" Cody asks. I'm not sure if he's asking what the word means or how it applies to the headline.

"Well, they called him disabled and then described how he threw himself off a bridge to save someone's life." She smiles at me, and I smile back so widely I can feel a tugging sensation where the glue is trying to hold my sideburns on.

"Yeah, pretty stupid," I add to the conversation brilliantly.

"I agree. All those guys making a big deal because some guy on the swim team managed to save someone by swimming." Cody shakes his head. I wonder if he's been talking to Ricky recently.

"You're on the swim team?" Sophia's eyes flicker over my legs in surprise. I guess she was focused on Cody when we talked about this yesterday.

"They *both* are," Clare says, glaring at her friend, who obviously wants to ask questions but isn't sure how. A lot of people I meet for the first time don't seem to be able to just talk to me naturally the way Clare and Cody both did. They either get too personal asking about my legs or they take the invisible wheelchair approach, trying so hard to be politically correct that they just pretend not to notice it at all.

"He's not as good as I am, seeing as I'm the captain and all…but he's in the top five of swimmers who *aren't* me," Cody says helpfully. "Of course, there are only six guys on the team so that doesn't mean much." He laughs. Sophia looks a bit shocked. I crumple up my program and throw it at him. It misses, dropping down onto the floor. Clare picks it up and beams it at him, making him laugh harder as he bats it away with his shield.

"You guys need to either move it or get out of line," an angry voice comes from behind us.

"Hey, chill out. We're moving. Have some respect. We have a real-life hero with us," Cody says to the giant-sized Deadpool standing behind us.

"Whatever. Just keep moving, asshole."

"Cody, just do it," I tell him, trying to avoid bloodshed.

"All right, all right. Keep your pants on!" We all move forward. I can't blame the guy behind us for being upset seeing as we've made it to the front of the line now and we're holding everyone up.

We get our autographs, which isn't nearly as exciting as I expected it to be. Being handed a piece of paper by someone in full costume, who may or may not be the actual actor and doesn't even say a single word to any of us, isn't exactly the highlight of my day.

"Time to eat, I think," Cody announces, staring at his autographed picture like it's the Holy Grail. My stomach definitely agrees. The stale muffin I ate this morning has long since become a distant memory.

We head down to the arena so we can hit the food trucks. I sneak a look at my phone, hoping that Cody doesn't notice. I'm really trying not to worry about Jack.

"Do you need any help navigating in here?" Clare asks as we come into the room. It's a lot more congested than yesterday, with bodies and tables jockeying for position on a floor that has basically disappeared under all the legs. There's a jumble of colored asses directly in front of me, and it's going to be tough getting through the crowd without running into or over something. Cody is usually the one who offers to get me through this sort of mess but he's already tunneling his way through the crowd, with Sophia following close behind him. He's probably forgotten we're here.

Should I be all manly and tell her I can do it myself and risk pissing off some super villain by running over his feet? Or do I suck it up and let her help? Which one would keep things comfortable between us?

I take a deep breath.

"Okay. Thanks. That would be great!" I yell it at her, emphasizing the last word. I seriously have to stop with the demented cheerleader routine.

Clare doesn't seem to notice as she takes control of my chair. I actually see the Batman Jack told me about as we thread our way up toward the food, and we exchange a quick smile.

"What do you feel like eating?" Clare asks as we scan the options.

"I'll have whatever you have."

"I like sausage and sauerkraut. Lots of sauerkraut." She moves into the lineup, letting me take over my own motion. It takes a while to get our food and it's so noisy right here that talking isn't really an option, so we just wait quietly. Clare smiles at me every once in a while. It's the best smile I've ever seen.

"So, let's find somewhere to eat." Cody arrives just as we get our food. He's holding a cardboard box full of hamburgers and fries.

"How many people are you feeding?" I ask him. He just laughs.

"We need to find a table. I don't want to eat standing up and I don't think we can all sit on Ryan's lap," he says, instead of answering me.

I get a sudden image of Clare sitting on my knee, eating her lunch as I wheel her around the room to the sound of romantic music and say intelligent things that make her smile sweetly.

"Here, you hold the food and I'll drive," Clare interrupts my vision while I sit there with a goofy grin on my face.

We move toward the tables in the dim hope of finding a few spaces to squeeze into.

"Oh, perfect! I know them," Clare says as she veers left and heads over to a spot by the wall that's crammed full of loud, colorful people, who are all filling their faces and talking at the same time.

And right there in the middle of them is Jack.

He's sitting quietly, looking around the table with a small, shy smile. He doesn't exactly look like part of the crowd, but he doesn't look unhappy or bored like he did yesterday either.

"Hi!" I say to him as we approach, trying not to sound too relieved. He looks at me warily, probably expecting me to bitch him out for not texting me or something.

He *did* say he would text. And he *didn't* do it. But I'm keeping my mouth shut this time.

"This is cool! I didn't realize that your friend was hanging out with some of mine, although I shouldn't be surprised. Bainesville is pretty small," Clare says to me, looking pleased.

She walks up to the guy sitting beside Jack at the end of the table and gives him a big kiss on the cheek. He's not in a character costume, at least not one that I recognize. He's wearing a hot-pink, shiny-looking shirt under a black vest that's covered in colored button things that sparkle in the lights. He's got earrings in both ears that match his shirt. His eyes are blue with heavy black makeup outlining them in a way that makes them jump out of his face. Right now they're jumping out at Clare.

"Hey! Can we squeeze in here with you guys?" Clare asks as he grins at her. The guy…or someone I'm pretty sure is a guy…sitting across from him grabs Clare and pulls her over to his side and down onto his lap, which is covered in white leggings that sparkle even more than the colored buttons do. He's also wearing a tight white top under a fur-lined cape. His hair is a flowing white wig. Clare giggles as she lands.

"You look gorgeous! Emma Frost is a good look on you, Lucas," she says, helping herself to a couple of the fries sitting in front of him. She looks over at me.

"Ryan, come and meet my brother Lucas and a few of our friends!"

Her brother? Seriously? I put what I hope is a cool expression on my face.

"Hi. I'm Ryan." My voice drops down to a lower pitch

than usual as I reach over to shake his hand, wondering if it's the right move. His fingernails look like shimmering silver talons. I hope he doesn't impale me with them. He grabs my hand and gives it a hard shake that I feel right up to my shoulder, staring at me with eyes almost hidden by the longest, thickest eyelashes I've ever seen.

"Oh, so *you're* the guy!" he says, as Clare slaps her hand over his mouth.

"Lucas, shut up!" she says, flushing a little. Lucas just laughs and pushes her hand away.

"Oh, don't worry, I won't embarrass you. *Much.* Come join us. This is Owen," he says, pointing at the guy in the vest. "And this is Caleb." He gestures toward the guy sitting beside Jack, who definitely doesn't look like Wonder Woman today. He's wearing jeans and a black T-shirt that shows off some impressive muscles that obviously weren't sewn into his shirt like Cody's. His hair is buzzed right down to the skull so I can't even figure out the color. He has that unshaven thing going on that would take me about a month without gluing on fake facial hair. He smiles slightly, giving me a little two finger salute.

"You're Jack's friend," he says, glancing sideways at Jack. "Nice to meet you." He sweeps his arm across the table. "This is everyone else."

They all wave or smile at us. Jack looks a little shocked by the two-worlds-colliding situation.

Clare is smiling happily at her brother. "I figured we'd run into you guys eventually. I think half the population is crammed into this place today."

"Yeah, the weird and wonderful half," Lucas says, making her laugh. Clare doesn't seem to think her brother is weird at all. Just wonderful. She's looking at him like he's her favorite person in the world.

Which gives me a quick stab of jealousy that's too stupid to think about.

There are probably a dozen people here. Mostly guys but a few girls also. Some are dressed...normally, I guess, although I'm not sure what that means anymore. The rest are about half-and-half split between character costumes I recognize and the way that Owen guy is dressed—as in, the kind of clothes that would make people at home stare and point and wonder what the hell is going on.

Which reminds me.

I look over to where Cody is standing and staring around the table, eyes wide behind his mask. Sophia has already found herself a spot at the table and is beckoning to him to join her. He looks like he can't move, feet glued to the floor for a change, as he tries to figure out what he's supposed to do next.

I guess Captain America doesn't have all the answers after all.

TWENTY-FIVE

It's fun watching Cody try to decide how to fit in with this particular crowd. No one is paying much attention to him except for Sophia, who alternates between stealing food from everyone and calling her hero over to cuddle with her.

Jack is far enough away from the spot I managed to squeeze into that we can't have a conversation. Every once in a while he looks over at me with suspicious eyes, even though it's obvious that I'm only here because Clare is. I'm definitely the follower in this relationship.

Not that we have a relationship. I just met her yesterday. She probably sees me as an interesting guy who's here today and gone tomorrow.

I watch her talking with her brother and everyone else at the table. Even though her costume has no sequins or brilliant colors, she's the brightest person here, almost as if there's some kind of spotlight shining down on her. Everyone smiles at her, like she's their little sister.

Her brother catches me studying her and grins at me with silver lips. I feel my cheeks flare up enough that no makeup in the world could mask it. He grins wider and winks. I wonder if those lashes make it hard to keep his eyes open.

"Ryan, do you mind if I tell my brother about the news story on you?" Clare asks, leaning close to me so no one else hears, so close that I can feel her breath on my ear. It's warm and soft but it makes me shiver a little.

"Not here!" I shake my head so hard that my wig shifts. Clare looks startled.

"Okay. Sorry. I wasn't trying to embarrass you. I just thought he'd be interested." She looks apologetic. She shouldn't be sorry. I'm the one who lied to her.

"It's okay. I just would prefer to keep it between us for now," I say lamely, glancing over at Jack. I realize what I'm doing a split second too late. Clare looks at him and then at me.

"So, Ryan. I hear you're a jock," Lucas says loudly, before I can decide what I'm supposed to do next.

"Yeah, swim team. Just high school."

"What do you mean, *just* high school. Our team is the best in the county. We kick ass everywhere we go!" Cody finally gets his feet unstuck and comes over to the table. He goes over to Sophia, who leaps to her feet with a mega-watt smile and gives him her chair before sitting on his lap.

"Okay. Should I assume you're a jock too?" Lucas asks Cody, who nods proudly.

"Captain of the team!"

Jack rolls his eyes and I grin at him.

"Does Steve know about your promotion?" I ask Cody, who ignores me completely.

"He's not the captain?" Clare asks me, turning away from the speed eating display.

"Only in his own mind. Which is enough for him. He does boss the rest of us around, so I guess we feed into his delusions."

"I think he was a bit out of his element at first, but now he looks pretty comfortable," Clare says. We both watch him as he tells a joke that we can't hear the punch line to. I have a quick dose of panic, hoping that he is aware of his audience. I imagine he has a lot of really ignorant jokes up his sleeve that wouldn't go over very well here. But everyone laughs when he stops talking so I guess he's figured it out. Or was it just dumb luck?

"Yeah, Cody doesn't usually have any trouble talking to people. He's like a giant human magnet most of the time."

"Jack seems a bit shyer, but he looks like he's having a good time." Clare's right. He's looking like life is a lot more interesting today than it was yesterday.

"He's pretty shy compared to Cody. Then again, most people are. Speaking of Cody, I think we should get him out of here while the going is good. I'm not sure how funny the next joke will be." Clare looks at me curiously. I just shrug my shoulders and smile. I don't want to tell her that I'm afraid the next joke will feature words like *fag* or *dyke*.

"We're going to head off now. Nice to meet you," I say to Lucas. He reaches over and shakes my hand again, holding it just a bit longer and tighter than he has to.

"Nice to meet you too. Take care of my little sister," he says, as she play punches him in the arm before kissing his cheek.

I push back from the table and wheel over to Cody.

"We don't have a lot of time left. I think we should go check out a few more things." I have to shout to make myself heard over whatever loud story he's telling. He stops talking and looks at me as if he's surprised I'm still here. He takes his phone out and looks at it.

"Shit. You're right. We'd better motor." He lifts Sophia off his lap and stands up. He does a knightly bow to everyone at the table, which makes them laugh. I go over closer to Jack.

"Do you want to come with us?" I ask him, trying not to shout. He looks at me for a second and then over at Caleb.

"Um. No. I think I'll just stick here for a bit. I'll meet you at the end of the day."

I nod, biting my tongue so I don't ask him if he's okay or if he needs anything.

We say our good-byes and then head off into the hallway, stopping every thirty seconds so that Cody can get a selfie with each character that interests him.

A couple of people even asked if they could have a selfie with me today, although I'm not sure if that's because they thought I was a kick-ass Wolverine or because of the novelty factor. I guess it doesn't matter. I said yes, which was definitely the right answer because both times Clare sat on the arm of my chair and put her arm around my shoulder.

"So, have you thought much about what you want to do after high school?" Clare asks me. We're waiting in yet another lineup. This time it's to have our pictures taken with the one star they could get to come here from Cody's favorite sci-fi show. I don't think either of the girls even knows who the guy is, and the show isn't one of my favorites, but apparently there was a vote, and Cody's pick won. I'm pretty sure Cody is the only one who voted.

"No. I mean, I want to go to college. But I'm not sure what for. I've even thought of coming here to Bainesville U." *Especially now.*

"It's a pretty good school. But I'm applying all over the place. I think I'd like to go away to school. But I still have two more years of high school so I have time to think about it. I love science. I think I'd like to be an astrophysicist."

"That sounds impressive. Then again, I'm not sure what an astrophysicist even does." *Playing the stupid card. Impressive.*

"It's basically using physics and chemistry to figure out where the stars and planets and all the other objects floating around in the universe come from. Like the big bang theory."

"I love that show!" Cody interrupts, holding his phone up and taking a picture of the lineup. Clare just laughs.

"Me too."

"I think Cody wants to be an Avenger when he finishes school," I say to her.

"I think he wants to be one right now." We watch as he runs up and down the line, taking pictures and talking to everyone he meets. Sophia is watching him too, the look in her eyes making it very clear that he's already her hero.

I wish Clare would look at me like that.

"So, why are we in this lineup again?" she asks, looking at the bodies snaking toward a very distant doorway.

"Mostly because Captain America told us to," I tell her, making her laugh again. I like making her laugh.

We keep chatting and watching Cody for another twenty minutes before finally getting our chance to have a two-second photo shoot with an actor that only one out of the four of us is even remotely interested in. We wait around for the printed photos, which we have to pay for even though Cody is the only one who wanted them. By the time we finish all that, it's actually time to get ourselves out to the car and head for home.

"I can't believe you have to go already!" Sophia says sadly, holding on to Cody's arm.

"Well, I'd stay longer, but young Ryan here has an early bedtime so we have to go," he says, smiling sweetly in my direction. I offer him a suggestion with my middle finger, quickly putting it back down when I see Clare notice. She just grins.

"Right. I've heard that Captain America is in bed every night at eight so he can be refreshed to fight crime in the morning," she says.

"He might be in bed by eight but he isn't alone," Cody says, wiggling his eyebrows at Sophia. She punches him on the arm.

"Cody! Don't be a pig," I tell him. I don't want Clare to get a bad impression.

"Ryan! Don't be a prude." Cody says as he and Sophia both laugh.

"It was really nice meeting you both," Clare says, looking mostly at me. "We should keep in touch."

"Sure. We can do the Facebook friend thing," I say, because it's the only thing I can think of. Cody gives me a quick punch on the shoulder. I ignore him.

"That would be nice. Here, give me your phone. I'll give you some contact info." As I hand her the phone, I see Cody grab Sophia and plant a huge kiss on her lips. She puts her arms around his neck and kisses him back.

"Here you go." I quickly pull my eyes away from Cody's lip-lock and smile at Clare as she hands my phone back.

I would love to kiss her good-bye. But it's a little difficult to figure out how to do that from down here. I can't exactly grab her by the arm and pull her down to my level so I can plant one on her. I don't want to ask her to lean down so I can kiss her because it'd be totally embarrassing if she said no.

If she wants me to kiss her, she pretty much has to be the one to initiate it.

"There's your friend. I'll go over and tell him you're here," Clare interrupts me as I sit here thinking about kissing her instead of actually talking to her. I look over to where she's pointing. Jack is walking across the room with Caleb and Lucas. Clare runs over to the three of them and I can see her talking to Jack and gesturing over to us. They all come back across the room, Clare sandwiched in between her brother and Caleb.

"Take care, Jack," Caleb says, putting one hand on his shoulder briefly.

"Thanks. You too," Jack says.

"It was nice meeting you kid," Lucas says to him. Then he turns to me. "Good meeting you, too. Good luck with your swimming." He stares at me under his giant lashes for a few seconds and then turns away to say good-bye to Cody, who has finally let go of Sophia.

"What are you standing around for? We have to go!" Cody says to us before sprinting toward the door without another glance behind him.

"*Standing* around?" Clare mouths at me, her eyes sparkling a little. I laugh—even though saying good-bye to Clare makes me feel more like crying—and head out the door with Jack so that we can leave the fantasy factory and get ourselves back to the reality that is Thompson Mills.

Great.

TWENTY-SIX

"Well that was seriously awesome. I can't believe we're going home already," Cody says as we head down the highway. "Next time we go, we're doing the whole four days."

"You think it'll ever come back to Bainesville?" I ask.

"Probably. The place was packed. It would have brought all kinds of money into a place that small."

"I guess you're right. I'd definitely go again."

The day *was* great. Everyone was incredibly nice, and we were accepted as if we were long lost friends. No one laughed at my costume, at least not to my face. And Clare said I looked fierce.

"Of course you would," Cody says. "You actually talked to a girl without spitting on her or falling out of your chair. I don't know if it's the costume or being out of Thompson Mills for a change, but you were like an actual guy today."

Jack snorts a little in the back seat. He's beginning to sound like Cody.

"Thanks. It's been one of my lifelong goals. To be an *actual* guy." I smack Cody on the back of his Captain America helmet. I took the time to wash my face and change my clothes but he's sitting there in full costume. I think he might even sleep in it tonight.

"You can be sarcastic all you want. Clare was into you. And it's not just because we were at Comic Con. I was mostly kidding about that. It's because you decided to talk to her like a real person."

"Which I guess is pretty ironic seeing as I was pretending to be an X-Men character from a fictional alternate universe."

"Whatever. It doesn't matter. You actually talked to her and made her laugh. And she didn't care about your stupid chair. I'm pretty sure she forgot it was there."

Cody's right. I did feel like an actual guy who can talk to girls today. I don't know if it was the costume or the environment that did it, but I didn't feel awkward around Clare at all. We discussed all kinds of different things, and she laughed at my jokes even if they weren't particularly funny. I laughed at hers, too, but they were all funny. She's ridiculously smart.

But Cody's wrong about one thing. Clare didn't forget about my chair. She talked about it like it was just a normal part of the conversation. A normal part of *me*.

"I still think the costume was a pretty good distraction. And it doesn't really matter what happened here anyway. The girls at home know me as the guy in a chair." Not that I care about the girls at home so much anymore.

"I don't think your costume was the distraction. The fact that you finally remembered how to speak was the only thing distracting Clare, so there's no reason you can't do that at home too. But you just think what you want. You can still be a lonely little nerd boy at home and talk to girls once a year when you go to Comic Con."

"Yeah, well maybe when I go away to school it'll be different and I'll have so many girlfriends I won't be able to keep track of them." *Or maybe just one girlfriend who's waiting to become a rocket scientist.*

"You just keep thinking that. I'd rather have the girlfriends right now, instead of waiting a year."

"So would I. Girl*friend* anyway."

Not much chance of that though. I really wanted to say something, *do* something to let Clare know how amazing I think she is. That I wished I could stay and get to know her better. But I didn't say anything. Just sat there and wondered about kissing her.

"You could if you weren't such a chickenshit. It's not like Bainesville is that far away. Clare liked you and all you did was ask her to *do the Facebook thing*. Seriously lame!" Cody says, laughing at me.

"Well, I'm just taking it slow. She's a lady."

"Right. *That's* why you didn't kiss her good-bye. Not because you're a scared little boy."

I just ignore him. He wouldn't understand anyway.

"How was the rest of your day, Jack?" I turn around so I can see him and hopefully find something else to talk about.

"Fine," he answers, staring out the window.

"I can't believe that Clare's brother knows Caleb and all your other new friends." He glances at me for a second.

"They're not my friends. I just met them. I'll probably never see any of them again. *New friends.* You sound like my mother on the first day of school." He's defensive, almost angry with me.

Cody glances at me quickly with a *what-the-hell* look on his face. I agree. I wasn't acting like anyone's mother. Not this time anyway.

"I didn't mean anything stupid. I just meant it was nice that you met some people like..." I don't know the right way to end that sentence.

"Like me? Because some of them are gay? That makes them *like* me? Seriously? Are you *like* every other straight guy?"

He's back to staring out the window. Why is he so pissed with me? I thought he had a good day. Is he mad that we crashed his lunch party or something? I don't get this.

"Of course not," I say. "I didn't mean that either. I don't know what your problem is!"

"Of course you don't. Just leave me alone, okay? I don't want to talk."

"Fine. Whatever." My stomach jumps a little at the tone in his voice. I've heard it before, but I don't know why it's there now.

I turn around and stare out the front window, wondering what the hell is happening in the back seat.

"So, what are you going to do about Clare?" Cody asks, acting like he didn't hear my conversation with Jack.

"I can't exactly have a relationship with her. She lives three hours away. It's not like I have a car or anything."

"So what? You only have a year left of school before you can move there. In the meantime, you can just lust after her from a distance and send her dirty texts."

"Yeah, right! That really sounds like me." Cody just laughs. "But seriously, I am thinking of Bainesville U after high school. It's just far enough away to give me some independence without Mom showing up with fresh underwear on a daily basis."

"I'd love for my mom to show up with fresh underwear when I move out," Cody says. "I'd be doing her a favor. Moms love doing the laundry."

I imagine my mother's face if she heard him say that. It makes me laugh. "Yeah, my mother is always begging me for clothes to wash."

"Anyway, Clare is the first girl that actually seems to think you have a brain. I wouldn't give up so fast if I were you. Then again, I'm Captain America. I never give up."

Cody does a salute, which is probably directed at himself instead of me, and focuses on the road for a while in silence. We stop for coffee about every forty-five minutes so that Cody doesn't fall asleep at the wheel. I'm pretty tired but I'm forcing myself to stay awake so I can poke him if he looks like he's drifting.

Jack doesn't get out of the car, not even to go to the bathroom. He's just sitting back there staring out at nothing. Maybe he's sleeping. I don't know, but I'm afraid to ask in case I make things worse.

Did something bad happen during the afternoon? Did some- one say or do something to him?

"Turn on the radio and crank it up. I need some tunes to keep me moving." Cody derails my train of thought by smacking me on the arm.

"Okay, keep your hands on the wheel so we all keep moving."

I do what he asks, trying to find a station with music that he'll like. He keeps shaking his head as I flip through.

"There! Perfect," he finally nods as I find the loudest, most obnoxious song on the radio. We spend the rest of the trip listening to Cody sing along to his music in the world's worst voice.

Jack's mother is standing at the window when we pull up in front of his house.

"Do you think she's been there all weekend?" Cody asks, looking at Jack in the rearview mirror.

"Probably. She's texted me about fifty times." Jack speaks for the first time in hours as he digs around for his stuff.

"At least you know she cares," I say to him.

"Right. Or doesn't trust me."

"I don't think too many mothers trust teenagers. It's a parenting rule. My mom always tells me she trusts me but she keeps pretty close tabs. She didn't text fifty times but at least ten, which for her is a huge number." I'm babbling but I can't seem to stop myself. Jack ignores me.

"Anyway, thanks for the trip," Jack says in a monotone as he gets out of the car.

"Yeah, no problem," Cody says. "Um, Jack?"

"What?"

"Now that we're home…I still have your back and everything, but you know, my friends aren't exactly as…understanding as I am so…" He trails off, actually looking embarrassed, which may be a first. He should be. If he's saying what I think he is.

"It's fine. I won't run up and kiss you in the halls or anything." Jack slams the door and heads up the pathway to his house without looking back.

Cody pulls out. I stay quiet because I don't want to get in a fight with him.

"Don't get all silent treatment pissed off with me, Ryan. I was nice to the guy. Nicer than you in some ways. At least I didn't go all nuclear mother hen on him. I've got a reputation. He has one, too, and it doesn't go with mine. It is what it is." His voice is defensive. Another first.

"I'm friends with him. I don't hide it. No one cares." I'm staring out the front window because if I look at him I might punch him.

"Well that's nice for you. You're not me. Your rep is different." If he wasn't driving I think I *would* punch him.

"Are we talking about my chair without talking about it now? Are you saying it's okay for me to be friends with Jack because I'm the crip and he's the gay guy?"

His head whips sideways as he looks at me for a second, eyes completely pissed, before turning back to the road.

"That's the biggest pile of bullshit you've ever said. You know perfectly well I didn't say that. You did. I don't ever call you a crip. I don't even think about it, and you know that. You're being a jerk."

He's right. Not about the jerk part. But the rest of it is true. And I do know it.

But he's being the jerk right now. Deciding he can't be Jack's friend because it might make trouble with the other guys he hangs around with.

Even though it's true. Which sucks. But he should still be better than that.

No wonder Jack ended up in the river. It's hard to stay grounded if you can't see any future that doesn't make your life feel like hell.

We pull up in front of my house in silence. My mom is also standing at the window, watching for me. Cody gets out of the car and grabs my chair.

"You can be friends with Jack. It doesn't mean I have to be. And it doesn't mean *we* aren't friends," he says as he helps me get out of the car.

"I know. It's fine. I just feel bad for the guy." It isn't fine, but I'm too tired to argue anymore.

"Believe it or not, I do too. I just don't think I can do anything about it." I look at him for a second. He actually thinks he hasn't done anything wrong here.

"I don't *believe* it at all. I don't think you feel anything for him. I think you're only worried about yourself. Like always. You really don't give a shit about Jack. If you did, you would do something about it."

"And what the fuck do you expect me to do?" He's standing

there holding my bag, looking as angry as I've ever seen him. As angry as I feel.

"What is it you always tell me? Be more confident like the great Cody McNeely? If you were really as confident as you say you are, you wouldn't give a shit about what anyone thinks of you. You wouldn't treat someone like crap just to protect your reputation if you actually believed in it."

I reach out my hand to take my bag from him. He shoves it at me, looking like he's going to say something. Then he just shakes his head and gets back in his car, slamming the door.

Captain America squeals the tires as he drives off into the night to protect the innocent from evildoers or whatever it is that fake Avengers do.

TWENTY-SEVEN

"So, how are things going with Cody and Jack?"

Clare looks at me from my computer screen, eyes all soft and concerned. I really want to reach out and touch her cheek, pretending I'm doing it in real life, but she can see me, which would make it kind of creepy.

It seems that Cody was wrong about how badly I left things with Clare because two days after we got home she messaged me, and we started talking. After a few days of writing to each other, Clare suggested that it might be nicer to do video messaging so that we could see and hear each other as if we were actually spending time together.

Might be nicer to actually see that beautiful face looking at me?

The first time we scheduled a time to video-call each other, I had a sudden urge to contact Jack and get him to make my

211

face up again. I wasn't sure if Clare remembered what I really look like.

Except that Jack is still barely talking to me. We've seen each other about three times in the past several weeks. He's always polite without being exactly friendly. I'm afraid to ask him anything just in case I send him spiralling off to some place darker than the one he's already returned to.

Turns out I didn't need his help with Clare.

"I love red hair!" was the first thing she said when she saw the real me again.

"I think freckles are so cool. Much more interesting than boring expanses of plain skin."

I'm pretty sure I'm in love.

Recently, I've started telling Clare about all the strangeness that is my life now that I'm back home. It's hard to believe that she finds my personal drama festival even remotely interesting, but she keeps asking about it, so I keep talking.

I stayed mad at Cody for a lot longer than five minutes this time. I'm still upset with the way he treated Jack, but we've somehow managed to find a way back to a kind of pseudo-friendship again. Mostly because he just kept on calling and offering to work on my swimming with me, and I eventually caved. So now we swim and talk about nothing in particular and pretend we're okay.

"Jack still isn't saying much. Cody is acting like everything's fine even though he hasn't said one word to Jack since we got back. I know you probably think that's sick."

"No, I get it. Lucas had trouble with all kinds of people

when he first came out after high school. Lots of people were supportive, too, but some so-called friends he'd had his whole life would look the other way when he came down the street. He was threatened by people he knew from kindergarten. It was really rough for a while. People get…afraid, I guess…when things change." She gives me a sad smile.

"Cody acts like he isn't afraid of anything or anyone most of the time. But he's obviously scared shi—I mean, scared to death of what would happen if someone figured out that Jack is actually gay and that Cody spent some time with the guy." Clare laughs at me.

"You can say shitless in front of me, Ryan. I'm not fragile."

"Sorry. My mother would offer to wash my mouth out with soap if she heard me curse in front of a lady." I tap my fingers against my lips.

"You're mom sounds sweet but very old-school."

"Oh, she's definitely old-school. Literally. She's the principal at *my* old school."

Clare laughs again. It sounds like bells. Not the old, rusty school bell my mother rings in my face. Delicate wind chimes gently catching a breeze on a warm morning in springtime… or something less embarrassing than that.

I'm glad Clare can't see inside my increasingly mush-filled brain.

"My mom is a judge. Probably lots of similarities between the two jobs."

"Yeah, I don't think we should get them together any time soon!" She looks at me silently for a few seconds.

"Maybe someday though," she says in a serious voice that makes my stomach dance around a little. In a good way.

"So, how's the swimming going?" she asks, changing the subject because I'm just sitting here with a stupid grin on my face.

"Not bad. Cody is still riding my…" I hesitate and she just raises her eyebrows. "…ass most days when he isn't busy, and I'm feeling good. Ready for the fall."

"That's great. I love to swim but I'm pretty slow. Maybe you could give me some pointers some day."

"Absolutely. I can give you some right now if you want!" This is actually something I know about.

"I meant in person. Together. In a pool." She shakes her head, grinning a little.

"Oh." I have to try not to stare as I instantly imagine her in a bathing suit. Her grin gets a little wider.

"Yeah, *oh*. And Ryan, I'm imagining you in a bathing suit, too, just in case you were wondering."

This time there's no makeup to mask my flaming red cheeks. I try to turn a little away from the camera so she doesn't notice.

"It's okay. You're super cute when you blush," she says, which just turns me into a three-alarm fire instead of a two. It makes her laugh. Wind chimes.

"You're seriously adorable, Ryan. My best friend, Karla, can't wait to meet you."

She told her best friend about me?

"You told your best friend about me?"

"Of course I did. Didn't you tell yours about me?" She arches both eyebrows into question marks.

"Cody is my best friend. He already knows." She probably thinks I could find a better best friend than someone who dumps people because they're gay.

"Anyway, Karla is dying to meet you. She wants to come online with us some time, but I told her she has to wait until we get together live and in person."

"I'm not sure when we'll be able to do that." I can't exactly ask Cody to drive me to Bainesville again. He forgot about Sophia about thirty seconds after we got home. He wouldn't drive there just for my sake.

"Maybe I'll get my brother and Caleb to drive me down your way some time. Caleb's been chatting with Jack, you know, giving him some ideas on how to find support networks. He might like to talk to him in person again."

I didn't know Jack was in contact with Caleb still. He never said anything to me. Then again, he never says much to me anymore.

I look at Clare for a second, trying to imagine the reaction of…well, pretty much anyone in Thompson Mills if Caleb or Lucas showed up in a sparkling pink shirt and makeup.

"Don't worry about it, Ryan. Caleb only dresses up for fun when there's a festival or something, and Lucas has jeans and plain shirts for camouflage when he needs it. No one will know."

I think about trying to persuade her that she didn't read my mind—or likely my face—accurately, but there's no point.

"I'm sorry."

"You can't be sorry for the attitudes of other people."

I think about my best friend. I feel like I should be sorry for the way he's acting.

"I guess. Speaking of attitudes…does your friend know about me?"

Her eyes get confused. "Karla? I already told you that she knows about you."

"Yeah, I know. But did you tell her about my chair?"

She looks at me, grinning a little.

"Well, seeing as you were sitting in it in the pictures I showed her, I didn't really have to say much." I look at her in surprise.

"You showed her pictures? Of me?"

"Of course I did. She thinks you're super cute. That's a direct quote."

"Oh." I can't believe she showed her friend pictures of me.

"Yeah, oh. Again. Anyway, she said you have great hair, gorgeous freckles, and a kick-ass body."

"That's probably not all she said."

"You need more compliments than that?"

"I don't mean that. I mean, what did she say about your… liking a guy in a chair?" My voice cracks in a very manly way on the word *liking*.

Clare looks at me for a long time, head tilted to the side, with big brown eyes that are like melted chocolate chips fresh out of the oven—or something less embarrassing than *that*.

"She asked a lot of questions. Gave a few opinions. I

answered the questions that were worth answering and ignored the opinions I didn't like. My opinion is the only one that matters because I'm the one who *likes* the guy in the chair."

And she smiles, a slow, sweet smile that makes my chest feel tight. My cheeks start to heat up again as she ends the call, and her picture fades from sight.

TWENTY-EIGHT

For the rest of the month, when I'm not talking to Clare, dreaming about Clare, or wondering when I'm going to see Clare, I spend my time working on my swimming so I can strengthen my shoulder and get my speed back to a point where I'm absolutely sure I'll be a full member of the team in the fall. It's my last year, and I don't want to miss a single swim meet.

I'm hoping to try out for the team in college as well, but I know the competition will be a lot fiercer. I definitely hold my own on the high school team, even in out-of-town competitions, but I'm still trying to prepare myself for the possibility that I'll be outclassed in a big school where kids come from all over the country.

Cody tells me that my attitude is full of shit. He doesn't see the irony in that statement.

Jack has been working pretty much full-time at the Supe.

I know he hates it but he hasn't had the guts to tell his mother he wants to apply to work somewhere else, so for now he's just putting up with it, waiting for the summer to end.

Of course, he hates school as much or more than working, so I'm not sure what he's got to look forward to. I hope Caleb has been helping him figure out how to make life more bearable. It would be really nice if Lucas did drive everyone here. It might do Jack some good to talk to those guys in person again.

It would do me a lot of good to talk to Clare in person again. My life is just weird these days. I could use an *actual* friendly face that doesn't have a computer screen in the way.

I pretty much only spend time with Cody at the pool, where he bitches at me about my swimming and cracks stupid jokes that don't seem to make me feel like laughing anymore. I see Jack down at the water sometimes, which is starting to feel more and more dangerous because he has been continuously down since we came home and still won't talk to me about it. I'm torn between wanting to stay away from the bridge completely and being afraid to let him be there alone.

So I keep going.

I don't think Cody even so much as acknowledges Jack's existence if he sees him anywhere around town. I know—at least I *hope* I know—that he would kick ass again if anyone ever tried to physically hurt Jack. But that's as far as it goes.

It is what it is.

It just isn't enough.

"Don't worry about it. He wasn't my friend before. He wasn't exactly my friend that weekend either. He tolerated me. Now he ignores me. I'd rather be ignored for being gay than attacked for it. It's fine." Jack shrugs his shoulders and looks down at the water. We're sitting on the bridge early in the morning, which is still the only time we come here. Most of the time these days we sit in virtual silence, but today I decided to bring up the subject of Cody to see if I could get Jack talking.

Which might not be the best plan I've ever had.

"It's not really fine, though, is it? How are things ever going to change if people like Cody keep acting like jerks?"

"Maybe it'll change someday, like a hundred years from now. Long after I'm dead and gone." He flings a stick at the water in an angry gesture. I resist the urge to grab on to some part of his body just in case he decides to follow it in. I wish we were somewhere other than on this bridge, looking at this river.

"Or when you move to Bainesville, alive and well," I say, trying to sound positive. He nods slightly. I watch him and think about what Clare told me about her brother and how hard it was for him when he decided to come out. Jack's life is already hard enough, and he's not exactly tough. I can't imagine how he would deal with the type of shit Lucas had to put up with.

Maybe if he moves away, he'll just have to stay there and never come back here to Homophobia Land.

"*If* I figured out how to move there some day, things could be okay. Maybe."

"But it's not okay now?" The answer is obvious, but I ask anyway.

"No, it's not. Nothing is okay now." He looks up at me, shading his eyes from the sun. After a few seconds, he takes a deep breath.

"When I was away from here, just sitting talking to Caleb and the others, I thought it would be. Okay, I mean. Everyone there was so positive, telling their stories and making me feel like it wouldn't be so bad, you know?" I nod even though I probably don't know.

"But the minute I got in the car to go home, it just all washed over me like I was back in the river and starting to drown all over again. My chest hurt just thinking about coming back here and facing another year or more of pretending to be someone I'm not. Imagining lying to my mom over and over again actually made me feel like I couldn't breathe. I hate not telling her who I am! It's just the two of us now. I should be able to tell her. But it scares me so much. I know she thinks that men marry women and that's it. She won't want me to be different. She probably even thinks it's a sin." He stops talking for a few seconds. I try to find something to say, but he starts again before I manage it.

"I *want* to tell her. I *need* to tell her. At least about being gay. I don't need to tell her about wrecking her skirt yet. One thing at a time." He smiles with his mouth but not his eyes. "I can't keep pretending to be someone else in my own house, but I don't know how to tell her."

"Did you ever ask Caleb about it? He likely already went through it, right?"

"Actually, I did ask. He said that he waited until he moved

away and had a support network in the city and was completely independent. He figured that way he'd have someone to turn to if his parents reacted badly, and he'd have somewhere to go if things went badly."

"Did it? Go badly?"

"I didn't ask. Didn't really want to know. But he seems like he's pretty together, although I don't know him all that well."

"So, if it worked for him, do you think maybe that's the best way to do it?"

He stares down at the water for a long time. He tosses a few more sticks, and we both watch them float away. Finally he looks up, his eyes dark and filled with tears.

"Maybe for him, but not for me. I can't stand it. It's literally making me feel sick all the time. I need to know she'll still be my mom, no matter what. I'll go nuts if I wait a year to find out." He wipes his hand over his eyes, trying not to cry.

This is awful every way you look at it. Jack shouldn't have to feel this scared. He should just be able to tell her, tell anyone he wants. He's not doing anything wrong. He's not hurting anyone.

Except he thinks he's going to hurt his mother.

This is making my head hurt. His must be ready to explode.

My mother was probably disappointed when the physio and surgeries didn't work enough to get me on my feet. She probably felt upset that she had to deal with wheelchairs and braces and hospitals when all she wanted was a cute little kid to bring up. But she's never said anything that would make me think any of those things. She's always been totally supportive, pushing me to try things, telling me I can be or do anything I want.

But what if I wanted to date guys? Would she be supportive about something like that? Would she still be proud of me?

I try to imagine her telling me she's disappointed and doesn't want me around because I don't want to marry a woman someday. I just can't see her doing it.

But I guess I don't *know* any more than Jack does.

"So, what are you going to do?"

He squints in the sunlight with red, damp eyes, which chokes me up a bit, even though I'm such a tough guy.

"I have to tell her. I have to know."

"Okay. Is there anything I can do?" I can't think of anything that would be remotely helpful. Jack's quiet for a while. I guess he can't think of anything either.

"Actually, there is. Could you come with me when I tell her?" He looks down, probably afraid to see my reaction.

Which is probably good because I can't trust my face right now. I definitely didn't think of that. There's seriously nothing I want to do less than sit there while Jack tells his mom something so personal.

But how the hell can I say no?

"Sure, I can do that."

"Really?" Jack looks shocked.

"Yeah, no problem." I try a smile to mask the lie.

"I don't need you to say anything. Just…be there. If that's okay."

No. Not okay. Uncomfortable. Awkward. Lots of other things I can't get my head around right now.

"Yeah, it's okay. I don't know how much help I'll be, but I can be there if you need me."

He actually smiles a little as he sniffs and digs around in his pockets, probably looking for a Kleenex.

How did I get into this?

I am seriously never throwing myself off this bridge again.

TWENTY-NINE

"I don't know how I can help him with this."

Clare looks at me sympathetically. I feel a bit guilty, like I've broken some kind of confidence with Jack by talking to her about this, but I didn't know what else to do. I can't talk to Cody or my mother about it, and if I keep talking to myself, I'm going to lose my mind.

I told her everything from the beginning. Even the lie I told about him at Comic Con. She just laughed at me and said she already knew about that part. Apparently I'm a shitty liar.

And a shitty friend. I told Jack I would come with him to tell his mom but now that he's actually told me that today is the day, I'm trying to find a way out of it. Instead of rushing over to help him prepare for the scariest moment of his life, I'm calling Clare.

"Just be there. Be someone for him to turn to if it goes

wrong. That's what I did for my brother." I look at her, surprised. I hadn't even thought about that.

"How old were you?"

"Fourteen. He was nineteen. I already knew. I think I always knew. But my parents didn't seem to. He wanted them to know, even though he was old enough to move out by then and could probably have just kept it a secret as long as he wanted to. But he told me he just had to know how they'd react."

"Yeah, that's kind of what Jack said. He just needs to know his mom still loves him. Does your mom? Still love your brother?"

She sits for a few seconds, obviously lost in a memory.

"Yes. Both my parents still love him. But my dad struggled a lot with the idea that his son is gay. He never suspected it at all. I think my mom did, so she wasn't as shocked. But Dad… well, it took a while. It's *taking* a while."

"But they didn't kick him out or anything."

"No, they never even thought about it. Not for a second. At least, I don't think they did. My mom sometimes even helps him accessorize now. Dad still prefers to see him in jeans and a hoodie, or maybe a football uniform if he could find one. One time Dad actually said that he didn't understand why Lucas couldn't be one of those gay men who are *masculine*."

She puts a major sarcastic spin on the last word. Clare is not a big fan of the words *masculine* and *feminine*. She says everyone should just be defined as a *person* without labels that dictate how we act or dress.

"What did your brother say to that?"

"Lucas just looked him straight in the eye and said, 'I'm more masculine than you could be in your wildest dreams… just ask my boyfriend.' Dad turned six shades of red and never mentioned it again." She laughs. "It took Lucas a long time to get to the point where he could say something like that and not worry about it. He's happy now. He has an awesome partner who my dad actually likes. They talk football together."

"Do you think Jack will be okay some day, too?"

"I have no idea. Whatever happens with his mom, he'll need friends to stick with him."

"Maybe he should wait to tell her until Caleb can come and be there for him. He'd be a lot more help than I would."

"That's not true. Jack asked you. You're his friend. You're the one he wants there."

"So you think I should go, even though I don't know what I'm supposed to be doing?" I was really hoping she'd tell me not to—that I'd be interfering or something. That I should find someone more responsible. Older. Wiser. Something.

"Obviously it's up to you, but I would go if it was my friend." Her chocolate eyes stare me down.

What choice do I have now?

"I guess I'd better get moving then. He's expecting me." She gives me a look that might make the next hour worth living, and then I shut down my computer, taking a deep breath before going to face whatever comes next.

I head outside and down the street, trying to ignore the heavy storm clouds that are rapidly filling the sky making the day so dark it seems like the world's about to end. A thunderstorm today would be a great example of pathetic fallacy for my English teacher.

Or maybe it would just be pathetic.

I arrive at Jack's within ten minutes. He's watching for me because he knows I can't get up the one cement step very easily on my own.

He comes out and pulls me up and into the house. His face is so pale that he looks like he did right after I pulled him out of the river. His mother is going to be worried before he even starts to talk.

"Where's your mom?" I ask him.

"She's on her way home from work. She had the early shift," he says, looking out the window.

"Maybe you should have some water or something to eat. You look like you're not feeling too well."

"I'd puke if I put anything in my mouth right now."

"Well, maybe you should splash water on your face or something. You're going to scare her before you even open your mouth."

He goes over and looks at himself in the hall mirror. He scrubs his hands over his face and looks again.

"I look like shit."

"Yeah."

"I'll try washing my face. I really can't eat right now." He walks down the hall, leaving me alone in the living room.

I look around. A beige couch sits against one wall, with a flowered blanket neatly tucked into the back and seat. A couple of comfortable-looking chairs and a coffee table. No TV in the room. I think they keep theirs in the family room at the back of the house. There are quite a few pictures on the wall above the couch. I wheel over and take a look.

Every photo is of Jack, starting from when he was a tiny baby right up to what must be his last year's school picture. It's like a photo gallery with him as the only subject.

I wonder if his mother has embarrassing videos of him like mine does.

"Better?" Jack comes back into the room. His face is now red and splotchy where he obviously scrubbed like he was trying to take the skin right off. His eyes look wet and red too. He definitely looks different, but I don't think *better* is the right word for it.

"Definitely." Seems like the right time to lie.

"Oh, shit. She's coming," Jack says, running to the window and then immediately stepping back out of sight as if he's playing hide-and-seek.

"Jack. You have to calm down. I'm sure it'll be fine. I've just been looking at the Jack photo display here. She's your mom. She loves you."

"She's my mom." He whispers it and closes his eyes for a second. They pop back open as we both hear the doorknob turn.

"Jack, I'm home," his mom calls out in a cheerful voice. Jack looks at me, his whole body trembling. I just put my hand up and shake my head, mouthing the words "It's fine." So helpful.

"In here!" Jack calls out, a little late as she's already coming into the room.

"Hi, sweetie. Oh hi, Ryan! I didn't know you were coming over." She smiles at me. She has a really nice smile.

"Yeah, Jack wasn't working today so I thought I'd come by." I smile back. Jack is just standing there, frozen in time and space.

"I wanted to tell you how nice it was that you invited Jack on your trip to Bainesville."

"It was fun. We'll probably go next year too, right Jack?" I raise my voice a bit, trying to get him unstuck. He looks startled. I don't think he's heard anything his mom or I said.

"Right," he says, nodding at nothing.

"So, can I get you boys something to eat or drink?"

"No, Mom. I actually have to talk to you about something." The words come out too fast and too loud. Jack closes his eyes for a second and takes a deep breath. His mom seems instantly worried. I don't blame her. He looks like crap.

"Honey? Are you all right? You don't look well. Is something wrong?" She puts her hand on his forehead, mom style. He reaches up and gently pulls it down and away.

"No, nothing's wrong. Not really. I just need to tell you something."

"Okay." She sits down, folding her hands in her lap like a well-behaved school kid, obviously trying to stay calm and look interested instead of worried.

I do the same because I don't know what else to do.

"I want to talk to you about what happened that day. At

the river." He looks over toward me. His mom takes a deep breath before nodding calmly.

"I'm listening."

Jack stands for a few seconds, looking at the pictures of himself smiling, riding trikes, digging in the sand, or sitting on a man's lap. I assume it's his dad. He stares at his own life for a while and then starts.

"I've been pretty…unhappy for a while. Confused about some stuff."

She nods sympathetically as if she knows what he's talking about. Maybe she does. Maybe she'll tell him she knew it all along and everything is going to work out all right.

"That day by the water, I was just…trying to do some thinking. You know? Figuring out who I am and what's going on with my life. How to keep going when it's so full of lies and…crap." He stops and takes a breath. His mom looks like she's going to cry.

"It was just so much. No one understanding me and what was going on."

"You could have talked to me."

"But I couldn't. That's exactly the point. I was afraid to tell you what was going on. Afraid of what you'd say. I love you. I didn't want to be someone who hurt you. I couldn't stand to think about it anymore."

"So you went into the water on purpose." She says it as a fact, not a question. It's obvious she already knew. A tear escapes and trickles down her cheek.

"I was just trying to get away for a while. You know?

Escape from everything. From myself." The last word comes out like a sigh.

"And from me? You can't go away from *me*, Jack. I'm your mother. It would break me to lose you." Another tear joins the first one, and she brushes it away impatiently as if she's pissed with it.

"I wasn't thinking about it that way. I was trying to… protect you."

"Protect *me*? From *you*? Parents don't need protecting from their children, Jack! I am so sorry that I did this to you. That *we* did this. I feel sick about it. I didn't realize how much the divorce had affected you. I know that some children see themselves as responsible when their parents separate, but I really didn't think you saw it that way. Your dad and I obviously didn't do this right, and it hurt you. I'm so, so sorry!"

"The divorce? You think this is about the divorce?" Jack has one hand on his forehead, rubbing it as if he's in pain.

"Of course. I should have known. And you don't have to try to protect me. I knew it was selfish to let your father leave. I knew it was against my vows. I should have tried harder. I just couldn't. I thought it would be better for you in the long run to have a peaceful house but I didn't think enough about how it would affect you later—now." She takes a deep, quivering breath. Jack shakes his head over and over again.

"It *is* better. I'm not a baby. I could see how unhappy you guys were. I was glad he left. He was angry all the time—with both of us. I didn't want you dealing with that. I didn't want to deal with it. This isn't about Dad or the divorce. It's about *me!*"

I'm wishing I was anywhere else in the whole world. I think both of them have forgotten I'm even in the room.

"What do you mean? Is something wrong? Are you sick?"

Jack looks at her and then at me. He smiles, but it's the most painful expression I think I've ever seen.

"No. *I* don't think so. Nothing is *wrong* with me. I'm not sick. I'm gay." His voice trembles. His eyes fill up with tears, but he rubs them away.

His mother sits perfectly still, staring at him. I can't read the expression on her face. It's like she's just gone blank, waiting for someone to fill her in.

"What?" Her voice is barely above a whisper.

"I'm gay. I've always been gay. I've had to hide it from you and everyone else since I was a kid. This is a really small town and people here aren't exactly accepting. I didn't know how you would feel, either, so I just hid. And I don't want to hide anymore." Every word is quaking, and the tears are dripping down his cheeks.

"What are you talking about, Jack? You aren't *gay*. I'm your mother. I would know."

"No, Mom. You wouldn't know. I got really good at keeping it from you. I didn't know how you'd feel, and I didn't want to hurt you."

"You're obviously confused, Jack. You can't be gay. You used to see that girl, Mandy." She's looking down at her lap as if there might be something written there that will explain what's going on.

"Mandy—Mandy *Wilson?* She was just my best friend…

when I was like, twelve!" Jack's voice is getting louder and higher.

His mother keeps her head down for a few seconds. When she raises it to look at him, her eyes have changed.

"You can't be gay, Jack. You're going to marry a woman and have children. We've always talked about that. You know that the church doesn't approve of anything else." Her voice is calm and sure, like she's solved the problem and just needs to explain it so Jack will understand.

"I don't need the church to approve! Just you." He takes a step backward.

I feel sick. This isn't going well at all.

"I can't *approve* of my only son destroying his chance at a normal life! You don't have to do this. You can decide who you want to be." She holds her hands out as if offering something to him.

"No! That's the point. This is who I am. I didn't choose it. I just *am* it. *You* have to decide to accept that." He is pleading with her as she just shakes her head again.

"I don't understand this. Did someone do something to make you believe this? Is it some kind of Internet thing trying to make young people believe they're something they're not? How did this happen?"

She bursts into loud, harsh sobs. Jack looks totally destroyed.

"It didn't happen. It just *is*."

"You need to get some help, Jack. We can find someone to help you figure this out," his mother says between sobs.

"To figure out how not to be gay?"

"To figure out how to understand that you can have a normal life."

"I *can* have a normal life. No one needs to fix me. I'm not broken! Please, Mom. I need you to understand!" He takes a step toward her, his hands out like he's a little kid who wants to be picked up.

She doesn't move. Just looks like she's never seen him before.

"Mom?"

She shakes her head at him, hugging herself and crying as if her heart just broke. As if her only son just drowned in the river.

He stares at her for a second and then runs from the room and out the front door. I sit there, expecting her to run after him but she doesn't. She just keeps crying.

Doesn't she get it? Doesn't she understand where he might be going?

I can't get out of here fast enough to stop him. What the hell am I supposed to do?

I grab my phone and send a quick text.

Jack's run away. Check bridge pls!

My phone vibrates back by the time I've wheeled my way across the room.

On it.

I head out into the hallway, but something stops me. I turn and look at Jack's mom, sitting on the couch, hugging herself instead of him.

"You're his mother. His *mother*. It's your *job* to love him!
No matter what. He was scared to tell you, but I told him it
would be fine. He's gone out the door, don't you see that? How
can you just sit there? He went into the fucking river once
because he was afraid. Where do you think he's gone now?"

I don't wait for an answer. I get outside and bump myself
down the step so I can head to the bridge. Cody should be there
by now. I hope he was fast enough.

The sky has opened up and water is pouring on my head
by the time I start down the sidewalk. Once I build up enough
momentum to take my hand off the wheels, I do the one thing
any independent, mature young man does in a crisis.

I call my mother.

THIRTY

I push down the wet road as fast as I can, ignoring the occasional twinge in my shoulder. I'm at the bridge in less than five minutes, and as I approach, I can see Cody's bike thrown down on the ground.

It's raining so hard that I can barely see, but I think I can make out bodies on the bridge, right at my "window." I start to push myself over, my heart pounding so hard that I swear I can actually see it through my shirt.

The storm is getting more excited by the second, with the wind joining in on the rampage, throwing sticks and leaves around while the river churns itself into a frenzy of waves that have scared away all the ducks. If Jack ends up down there today, I don't know if we'll be able to find him in time.

I finally get up to where I can see them clearly. Cody is standing in front of my window. Jack is trying to move around him while Cody feints left and right, stopping him from getting through like they're at some kind of bizarre football practice. It almost looks funny, and I have a ridiculous urge to laugh.

I swallow it hard as I approach. Neither of them notices me in all the noise and mess.

"You're not going in the river again! I'd have to jump in after you, and I'm already wet enough!" Cody yells at him, trying to hold on to the railing and block Jack at the same time.

"I don't want you to jump in. I didn't want Ryan to jump in. Everyone needs to leave me the fuck alone!"

"Jack!" I scream his name. He spins around.

"Go away, Ryan! I don't want you here!"

"Too bad! I'm not leaving. Neither of us is, so you might as well just stop it. You can't get past both of us."

"Why do you care anyway? I'm nothing to you guys. Cody hates me, and you just see me as a charity case. So back off!"

"That's just bullshit," Cody yells at him. Jack spins around toward the water again, trying to climb up on the railing. Cody grabs him and shoves him back toward me.

"I said leave me alone!" He's screaming and crying. "Just let me go, Ryan. You heard her. She doesn't want me!" He gives up suddenly and crumples to the ground, lying on his side as the water pours down on him. I move closer, trying to shelter him a bit. It's raining so hard that he could practically drown without going into the river.

"She probably just needs time. Old people can't figure things out as fast as we can," Cody says to him, still standing guard. He should still be carrying his shield.

"I knew she wouldn't understand! I shouldn't have told her. It's done. Don't you see? I've ruined everything! Now I can't go backwards!" Jack is crying and yelling at the same time. Cody reaches over and pats him gently on the shoulder.

"Yeah, well you sure as hell wouldn't be helping anything if you went forward right now because I would have to jump in after you and pull a *Ryan*. Which would piss him off because then he wouldn't be the big town hero anymore."

"Because *that* was so much fun," I say. Cody just snorts as Jack ignores us, drawing his knees up to his chest with both arms and rocking himself.

"Why did I tell her? I'm so stupid," he says.

"Sounds like she's the stupid one," Cody tells him. Jack gives him a furious look.

"Don't talk about her like that—she's my mother!"

"Right. She is. She'll figure it out," I say. "Cody's right. Adults are just slow to process things. She just needs time." The weather is getting worse, and I'm doing my best to outshout it, trying to make Jack hear me. Trying to make him believe me.

"Time for what? To accept me, or to decide she wants to kick me out?" he yells.

"I still don't think she'll kick you out." I say it, but I'm not sure anymore.

"So, she'll just try to cure me for the next year and make me feel like some kind of freak. I don't want to live that way." He sits up. Cody casually closes one hand on his arm. Jack doesn't seem to notice.

"Well, if it gets too bad, you can always stay with us until you move away," I tell him, really hoping that's true.

Jack thinks about what I just said. "Your mom would be cool with that?" he asks.

"I'm sure she would be."

He looks at me and then out over the water. I look too, blinking as the memory of staring down there desperately trying to find a yellow skirt flashes into my mind.

Jack raises his head. "But I don't want to live with you and your mother. I want to live with my own mother. I want to live with my own mother who wants to live with me. The *me* that I am, not the one she thinks I should be!" He starts to get to his feet and looks down at his arm, realizing that Cody has a hold on him. He tries to shake loose but Cody just tightens his grip.

Cody says something to him that I can't hear. Jack stops struggling and stands there, staring at the water.

What I *can* hear is the faint sound of cars over the thrashing rain. I see the lights of what I hope is my mother's car, along with a police cruiser with full emergency lights dancing. Both vehicles pull up to the bottom of the bridge.

Mom called the police. Great.

And now we're right back to the beginning of this particular story.

The officer gets out of her car first and comes up over the bridge. Officer Peabody. Of course, that's who would get the call. She doesn't say anything when she realizes Jack is here and Cody has him. She stands close and waits. Jack doesn't acknowledge her presence. He might not even know she's here.

I smile because I'm actually glad to see her this time.

I watch for my mom, but she's taking a while to get out of her car.

Cody is still talking to Jack, and I still can't hear them. Jack nods a little and then puts his hand over his face. Officer Peabody stands right beside him, one hand resting on the railing by Jack's side.

My mother finally gets out of the car. I try waving at her, but she doesn't wave back. She's still standing there in the relentless torrents of rain. *Why?*

A few seconds later she walks over to the passenger side and opens the door. Someone gets out. It takes me a second to realize that it's Jack's mom.

I look over to see if Jack has noticed, but he's still facing the other way.

Both of them come over to us. My mother bends down and hugs me, squeezing me tightly and kissing my cheek.

"Are you all right?" she asks.

"I'm fine," I tell her, which she knows is a lie. "How did you get her to come?" I nod toward Jack's mom.

"She was already halfway out the door when I drove up."

Jack's mom moves over to the railing, nods at the officer, and then touches Cody on the shoulder. He looks like he just might tell her to screw off. She speaks to him for a couple of seconds and then he lets go of Jack, moving away slowly, as if he doesn't trust that Jack is safe with his own mother.

I don't blame him.

"She was awful to him. She should have known better," I tell my mom. I can feel angry tears mixing in with the rain.

"She was…shocked. She wasn't thinking. She knows better now." It sounds like an excuse to me and not a very good one.

"Is she going to fix it? Make it okay with him? Is *he* going to be okay?" I ask, wanting her to tell me that everything will be all right the way she always did when I was little and something was upsetting me.

"She told me she'll do whatever it takes to make things right for Jack." I search her face to see if she's telling me the truth. I can't really tell because between her tears, my tears, and all the rain, her expression is pretty much washed away.

"Do you believe her?"

"Yes, I do, and that gives me hope that both of them are going to be okay. They'll need a lot of help along the way but I believe she does love him and wants the best for him."

"It looked like she was more worried about what's best for her. She shouldn't have treated him like that. He was trying, you know? Making plans. But he was so scared of her. And she treated him like shit." My mother nods and looks at me for a long time.

"I know. She was taken by surprise and handled it badly. It isn't right or fair but people…parents do that sometimes. *You* know that you don't ever have to be scared of me. You know that I love you. *Always*. Right?" She's holding me by the shoulders, looking straight into my eyes like she's trying to burn her words into them.

"Yes. I know." My chest feels like it's going to break wide open, but my mother grabs me in another tight hug that keeps me together.

She finally eases back and gives me another kiss. We look over to where Jack's mother has both arms wrapped around her son, holding him as tightly as my mother just held me. As we stand there watching, I see Jack's arms slowly come up and return the hug.

Cody comes over to us, and Mom gives him a big hug too. "Thanks," I say to him.

"Told you I had his back," he says, shrugging like it's no big deal.

We all stay there for what seems like a very long time as the storm whirls around us, trying to grab our attention. Jack's mom is talking to him, and every once in a while I see him nod. She never lets go of him for a second, just keeps on hugging and talking until we're all so wet that it feels like the water has started to seep through the skin, down into our bones.

Finally, the two of them turn around. Officer Peabody walks beside them as they come to the middle of the bridge where the rest of us are waiting.

Jack's mom forces herself to let go of her son and walks over to me. She stands looking at me for a few seconds with the same endless-pit eyes that her son likes to use on people. I start to get nervous that she's going to rat me out to my mother. I don't think Mom would be too impressed by the way I talked to her, even if everything I said was true.

In the end, she doesn't say anything at all—just wipes her eyes and gives me a tiny smile. Then she turns back and puts her arm firmly across Jack's shoulders, pulling him in close to her side.

Cody grins at Jack. "So," he says, "you better come by the pool one of these days. If you're going to keep hanging out here, I think it's time someone taught you to swim."

Every once in a while Cody manages to surprise me.

Jack also looks surprised for a second, but then he gives Cody a tiny smile before walking slowly across the bridge with his mother, neither of them looking back as they head home.

Cody comes up behind me and pushes my wheelchair to the other side of the bridge. I'm glad he can't see my face. I'm feeling a bit choked up at his offer to teach Jack to swim.

"You know, it actually kind of sucks that I didn't have to jump in after him. I'd like to try being an actual hero sometime and save someone from drowning, like *Super Ryan*."

And he's back.

I laugh as my mother looks at him with something close to shock. "I think you just did," I tell him. We keep on moving, putting the river behind us, while my mother stands in the rain and watches us go.

ACKNOWLEDGMENTS

As always, I need to express my overwhelming gratitude to Margie Wolfe and all of the staff of Second Story Press for their ongoing support of my writing these past eight years...even if that means rejecting a manuscript now and then so that I can go back to the writing board and create something better! Special thanks to Kathryn Cole for her instant faith in my little story and her patience with me during the whirlwind editing process that followed the quickest turnaround in my career, and to Kathryn White for helping me keep my names straight and making sure I'm not repeating myself.

My deepest gratitude to the grandmother who came to my signing last year and took the time to tell me about her young grandson who was about to learn how to use his first wheelchair. Ryan has borrowed some of your story to create his own and I sincerely hope that this book becomes only one of a very large and diverse selection of stories with characters that your grandson can relate to as he grows into a reader.

Finally a quick but heartfelt thanks to the many individuals and organizations dedicated to helping young people find a way out of the darkness back to a place of hope.

ABOUT THE AUTHOR

LIANE SHAW is the author of several books for teens, including *thinandbeautiful.com*, *Fostergirls*, *The Color of Silence*, and *Don't Tell, Don't Tell, Don't Tell*, as well as a work of non-fiction called *Time Out: A teacher's year of reading, fighting, and four-letter words*. Liane was an educator for more than 20 years, both in the classroom and as a special education resource teacher. Now retired from teaching, Liane lives with her family in the Ottawa Valley in Ontario.